# SEXBOT

Patrick Quinlan

A Strawberry Book

www.strawberrybooks.com

**IMAGINE**

ISBN: 098821380X
ISBN-13: 978-0988213807

"[A] thrilling ride that will keep you hanging on the edge of your seat. It will make you curse the fact that you need sleep." **-- Bullz-Eye.com**

"The story combines vicious villainy with threadbare morality to produce a bang that movie producers and script-writers would be sorry to miss. Once you've picked it up, it's hard to put it down." **-- Channel NewsAsia (Singapore)**

"THIS is the stuff – violent, pacy, stylish and funny." **-- The Daily Mirror**

"Quinlan delights in wrong-footing the reader. A fast-moving, hugely entertaining thriller." **-- The Observer on Sunday**

"[A] Leonardesque thriller. For this top-notch noir entertainment, think Coen Brothers (Blood Simple) in print." **-- Mystery Scene Magazine**

"Quinlan brings to glorious life several offbeat, deviant characters from roads less traveled. [THE FALLING MAN] hurtles along like an express train to its smashing climax." **-- Publisher's Weekly**

# FOR SARA

Trust in dreams, for in them is hidden the gate to eternity.

-Kahlil Gibran

THE FUTURE DOESN'T NEED US.

# CHAPTER ONE

The two men, killers, stood silent outside the high outer walls of the mansion, lingering among the palm trees.

Dressed in black, they looked like two wraiths, dark ghosts, hiding in the shadows. On this night, they wore hooded coats to protect themselves against the pouring rain. The raised hoods further obscured their faces.

They called themselves Mr. Blue and Mr. Green, but Mr. Blue's real name was not Blue. He was broad and muscular, and he was known for his bad temper. His body was scarred by countless battles. He had murdered dozens of people. His nose bent sideways as if punched by the hand of God.

Mr. Green's real name was, in fact, Green. He was tall and slim, with very fast hands. His face was unremarkable. He had a receding hairline. He looked like he could be an accountant, or a teacher. You wouldn't remember seeing him. He was logical and detail-oriented. He was also cold blooded and relentless.

For both men, killing was a job and, on this night, that job took them to this sleek, white stucco, four-story house on the coast. Only the twenty-foot high stone walls and state-of-the-art security system stood in their way.

Mr. Green opened a metal control box at the base of the wall, and made quick work of the latter, disabling the home's security cameras and electronic lock system, as Mr. Blue looked on. The two men had worked together before. Mr. Blue didn't much like Mr. Green's personality, but he appreciated his professionalism and his knack for the finer points of technology. It was a beautiful thing to witness.

Mr. Blue was less polished, but no less effective. Interrogation was his specialty. Compliance, restraint, and information extraction - that's how they described it in industry jargon. In regular English, it meant torture. He was especially good with reluctant subjects.

Those skills wouldn't be needed tonight. This was a straight contract kill, made to look like a break-in gone wrong.

He watched as Mr. Green closed the control box and nodded. The movement of Mr. Green's head was barely perceptible.

"You opened both doors?" Mr. Blue said.

"The wall and the house," Mr. Green said. "We're as good as in."

Mr. Blue went to the reinforced steel door set into the wall. He grabbed the giant decorative knob and pulled. The door came open easily. He smiled to himself and, just like that, he slipped inside the wall.

The two men walked across the grounds toward the house. The shimmering pool was to their right. It was a beautiful setting, with the Gulf of Mexico stretching to dark infinity beyond the seawall. The rain fell hard and fast, and struck the ground in fury. The pool water looked like it was boiling.

The house was to their left. Mr. Blue gazed up at it as they approached. From here, it was impossible to tell what shape it was. Maybe it was a triangle, maybe it was an arrow pointing to heaven. Some pointy-headed college boy with an auto-cad must have thought it made a statement. Certainly, it was contemporary. It was abstract. It was a piece of shit.

It was, he had to admit, a much nicer place than the one he lived in. These computer scientists made a lot of money.

Mr. Blue knew he should keep his mind focused on the job at hand, but he allowed himself a moment to muse about the last scientist they'd met.

He and Mr. Green had just visited him out on the west coast, at a cliff house near Big Sur. A guy named Martin Wacker - what an arrogant prick! Wacker had taken a little rest and relaxation trip out there. And they had come to see him during his holiday.

They had tied Wacker to a chair, forced him to drink bourbon at gun point, then sent him off the cliff in his Mercedes convertible.

Whoops! Drunk driving accident. People should drink more responsibly, especially on curvy mountain roads high above the ocean.

Before he went, Wacker had tried to buy them off. It spoke volumes about the kid that he thought such a thing was even possible. Blue remembered sitting in the living room of that fantastic cliff house, a little drunk himself, watching the sun sink below the ocean. He listened to this snot nose, bearded, four-eyed 32-year-old genius tell them about how much money he had, and how they could have it all, if only they let him live.

"We already have money," he told Wacker. "Lots of it."

Blue glanced at Green. Green stared straight ahead, his eyes blank, waiting until Blue gave him the word. He wasn't even listening. Hell, Green didn't care about money. He didn't care about anything but doing the job. He had all the money he needed. If he had any more, what would he even buy with it?

"In the drawer," Wacker said. His trimmed beard and his black framed Gucci glasses made him look like some kind of fake backwoodsman in a fashion magazine. With his head, Wacker indicated a glass china cabinet with a couple of sliding wooden drawers. "On the right. There's about ten thousand dollars in there. Cash. I brought it just to have some spending money. You can have it. Consider it a down payment."

Blue was wearing black leather gloves, as he always did. He went over to the cabinet and pulled open the drawer. A wad of cash sat there. He didn't bother to count it. He picked it up and put it in his pocket.

When he turned around again, he caught Green frowning at him. Green shook his head.

"What?" Blue said.

"It's a breach of protocol."

Blue shook his head in turn. Everything was a breach of protocol these days. Everything was against the rules. Don't touch anything. Don't take anything. Don't drink beer from the fridge. Don't steal the artwork off the walls. Don't blow up the safe. Where was the fun anymore? Hell, Wacker wasn't going to need the money.

Blue walked back over to the computer genius. He took the bottle of bourbon off the small side table, poured another double shot, and held it to Wacker's lips. Behind his glasses, Wacker's eyes went wide.

"Drink," Blue said.

Wacker's lips were trembling. "I don't want anymore."

With his free hand, Blue pulled his gun out of its holster. He put the business end to Wacker's temple. He would never shoot the man - this death was going to be an accident. But how could Wacker know that? He couldn't.

"Drink," Blue said again.

Wacker drank.

Before the end, before he passed out, before they bundled him into his pricey car and let him loose off the edge of the bluff and into the waiting arms of mother ocean below, Wacker started talking. He talked too much, in fact. It was drunken gibberish, and Blue hated listening to the ravings of dead people.

That, and Wacker was crying. Blue couldn't stand it when men cried. It didn't make him feel sympathy. All it did was piss him off. Blue came from that world where men didn't cry, and boys stopped crying when they were eight years old.

"Please," Wacker said. "Please don't do this. I know a secret…"

Blue was bored. He wanted to wrap the night up. Still, he raised his eyebrows. He liked secrets. Secrets often meant money.

"Okay."

"I have the secret to everlasting life. It's why they want me dead. I can give it to you."

"Martin," Blue said, "I have to be honest with you. That doesn't sound very promising."

"No, it's real. If you had this secret… Listen, it's incredible. The brain… it isn't what they think. The human mind is elsewhere."

Blue's mind was elsewhere. He held the glass to the man's lips again.

"Drink," he said.

Now, a week later, he and Mr. Green had reached the security door of the beach house in Florida – the house of Scientist Number Two. They paused by the door, and stood in the heavy downpour. The rain pattered on their raincoats, and ran in rivulets down their faces.

"Any sign of trouble, we blow her away," Mr. Blue said. "Alarms, panic rooms, anything like that, just boom. We don't want a protracted episode in there, and we don't want any uninvited guests. If there's no trouble, then it's just a break-in and we play it like that. You check her identity and I'll do the honors. We got it?"

Talking to Mr. Green was like talking to a cardboard box. Mr. Green nodded. "Got it."

Mr. Blue touched the door and pushed. It opened easily.

They went in.

\* \* \*

Inside the house, Susan Jones was afraid. So afraid, she could barely move.

With Martin dead, it was only a matter of time before they came for her. Oh, they said Martin had died in a drunk driving accident, but she didn't believe it. Martin drank, and Martin drove, but Martin didn't drink and drive. If Martin was drunk and he needed to go somewhere, he called a taxi.

Susan sat in her living room, listening to the heavy rain drum outside against the tall windows. She sipped from a glass of red wine. She could feel her heart beating through the wall of her chest. Her hand trembled as she lifted the glass to her mouth. The dark color of the wine made her think of blood, and of death.

She wore slacks and a dress shirt, pulled untidily from the waist of her pants. Her shirt was open three buttons, and her long hair, usually pulled back in a tight bun, hung loose and unkempt. Her feet were bare. When she came home, she hadn't bothered to change out of her work clothes.

She had gone to see Howard again today, and the guards had turned her away. Again. They told her that Howard had to fly out of town on business, but she could see it in their eyes. *Howard doesn't want to see you.* If Howard wouldn't see his star engineer anymore, it could only mean one thing.

Howard wanted her dead.

"Do something," she said, and the dry croak of her own voice startled her.

She glanced at the opulence of her surroundings. She had loved this house once. This living room was on the third floor. The white wraparound sofa she sat on cost ten thousand dollars. The five foot long abstract painting that hung behind it cost fifty thousand. The baby grand piano was a priceless antique - a gift from the company, because they knew her first love was music. The floors were polished oak. The floor to ceiling windows, on a clear day, would give startling 270 degree views of the beachfront and the Gulf of Mexico.

Tonight all the shades were drawn, and the place reminded her of a crypt.

She was still young, just 33 years old, and she was rich. Indeed, she was much wealthier than she ever imagined she'd be. Even when she graduated from the Massachusetts Institute of Technology a dozen years earlier, she hadn't yet imagined the money she would soon amass. But she'd grown rich doing something she never expected, and now there was a price to pay.

A flat black video monitor extended on a thin, flexible mount from the table in front of her. She pulled it closer for the tenth time tonight, and it came alive instantly. She tapped a few buttons on the touch screen, navigating to the bank of security cameras mounted outside her home.

Nine views popped up, laid out on a grid in front of her. Three of them showed various angles outside the walls of her home, all clear except for the rain, and the palm trees swaying in the heavy wind. Two screens showed views inside the grounds, including one of the in-ground pool, with its submerged blue light shining eerily up into the night.

Four of the screens were blank. Just a few minutes ago, they had been on. As she watched, one by one, the other five screens went blank in quick succession.

"Oh no," she said under her breath.

Her heart beat faster than ever.

Of course. It was easy for them. They could break the security with no problem at all. The company had built this house, a reward for her groundbreaking designs, and for all her hard work.

Suncoast Cybernetics had increased its revenues by a factor of ten, all because of people like Susan Jones, Martin Wacker, and a few others. All because the company was making robot sex dolls available to every wealthy man and woman, anywhere in the world, who wanted one. Each year, the robots became more lifelike, more intelligent, more amazing than the year before. And the newest designs, playthings for the ultra-rich, were the most mind-blowing yet.

Sexy? Yes, sexier than any woman alive. Incredible bodies, built to the customer's specifications. Athletic, smart, super-durable, human in every detail, save one.

They were more perfect than any human could ever be.

Once upon a time, she had been proud of the Sexbots. But the success had left her jaded, and restless. And truth be told, the Sexbots made more than a little ashamed. For a long time, she hadn't even told her mom and dad what she did for a living.

She remembered their reaction when she finally did tell them. Hyper-realistic sex dolls? Really? Is this what they had put her through school for? Is this how they had raised her? Is this what she should be wasting her God-given talents on?

It had caused a painful rift in their relationship that still hadn't healed. Once upon a time, her parents had been her best friends. Now? She barely spoke to them.

Worse, the company had taken the Sexbot technology and developed a line of robots for military applications. Killers. Assassins. All of them based on her work. She was irate when she heard of it, but there was nothing she could do. She had been paid for the technology, and the company held the patents.

Last year, she and Martin had struck out in a new direction, with the company's blessings, and they had stumbled upon a secret neither of them could ever have imagined. A possibility so gigantic that it would change the course of human history - a breakthrough that meant they would be remembered forever. And one which left them isolated and terribly vulnerable.

The company owned her. They watched her. They could breach her security system if they wanted. They could kill her if they wanted. And in the days since Martin had died, she had sat here frozen, helpless, becoming more and more convinced the company wanted exactly that. The company would kill them both, and not because they had invented robot sluts.

It was the new project. She and Martin called it Methuselah.

8

If that project came to fruition, and recent experiments with chimpanzees suggested that it already had, it would bring the company far more money than the Sexbots ever could. Suncoast Cybernetics was poised to become one of the richest and most powerful corporations in the world.

What was it worth if you could corner the market on immortality?

* * *


Mr. Blue pushed through the ground level security door.

Behind the door, a flimsy card table stood. Its thin legs were not quite fully extended, and so were not locked in the open position. The slightest touch could topple the table. On top of the table was a thin glass champagne flute, very fragile.

Three days before, Susan had bought the cheap card table at a discount store. The champagne glass was one of a very expensive set she'd had for years. She had taken to putting the table and the glass against the door when she came home at night.

When Blue pushed the door, it opened and bumped into the table. The table legs folded and the table collapsed to the floor. When the champagne glass hit the ground, it exploded like a very tiny, very lovely little bomb.

For a moment, Blue and Green stood looking down at all the sparkly shattered glass, and at the folded card table. Blue glanced around. In front of them was a flight of stairs leading up to the living quarters. Blue looked at the ceiling. It was textured stucco. He fancied he could hear the pitter-pat of running feet somewhere above his head.

"Shit," he said, and burst for the staircase.

* * *

Two stories above, Susan heard the table fall and the glass break.

She jumped from the sofa, spilling her wine across the bright white pillows. The red wine made a stain like a gunshot wound. She had no time to worry about it. She only had one chance, and a slim one.

She raced across the room to the spiral stairs. The top floor of this place housed her private lab. She was a workaholic, no time for relationships, and she often worked late into the evenings after she came home. Constant work was the key to her success, it was the key to life everlasting, it was the key to everything.

Below her, footsteps pounded up the stairs.

She grabbed the railing of the thin metal staircase. She pulled herself up the spiral, gasping as she did. She was not fast. She was carrying twenty extra pounds she had been meaning to lose.

She reached the top of the stairs. She heard little sounds, little frightened mouse-like sounds. They were coming from her own mouth. In a sudden flash of insight, she realized that the thing to do when Martin died was to buy a gun. Buy a gun and leave the country. But it was too late for that now. It was too late to do anything.

Down the hall was her lab. She floated there on legs that felt detached from her body. Her head felt like a balloon on a long tether. Her feet looked far away.

She reached the door. There was an electronic keypad lock. She started to punch in her combination, but her hand shook too much. She pressed the CANCEL button and started again. Then she noticed that the lights of the keypad weren't even on.

She stared at the blank keypad for several seconds. It took that long for the meaning of it to reach her fevered mind. The security cameras weren't the only system they had breached. The electronic locks were down, too.

Shit. They were shutting everything down.

She touched the door. It opened without a sound. She pushed through it, hoping that the overhead lights didn't go off next. She was scared, more scared than she had ever been. But if the lights went off, she would be terrified, maybe too terrified to move, or even think. The electricity was her only hope of survival.

If they shut the electricity off, she would no longer be able to do the one thing that might save her. It was a long shot anyway. And she needed power to do it.

The company was all-powerful. She knew now what Martin had already discovered. When the company wanted you alive, you were alive. When the company wanted you dead, you were dead. You belonged to them. The company gave you everything, and it could take away everything, including life itself.

But maybe not this time.

In the darkness of the room, a bank of lights illuminated the far wall. There wasn't much time, so she turned on the overheads. Hell, if there were killers in the house, they would find her soon enough. No reason to hide or pretend she wasn't in here.

She moved quickly. She barely spared a glance for the female robot - a Sexbot - that stood in a long plexiglass tube about five feet away. She merely verified that its power was on and its data drive was plugged in to the bank of servers.

Quickly, Susan tore off her own shirt and slacks, disrobing down to her bra and panties. She dropped the clothes on the floor.

She went to a monitor, punched through several interactive screens, inputting instructions she had gone through dozens of times before. Then she snatched a black remote control device from the desk.

She entered a large plastic-domed chamber, different from the one the Sexbot was in. This was the transfer tube. There was a white leather chair inside the tube. She took a deep breath and sat down in it. The chair had straps for arms and legs, but she didn't bother with them. The subjects of this procedure were usually chimpanzees, and they didn't often sit in this chair willingly.

Susan had done this many times with great apes, but never

before with the greatest ape of all, a human. It was a sort of poetic justice that she would be the first human trial.

With some luck, it might just work. God, she hoped so.

Either way, Susan Jones the computer scientist would probably be gone in a few moments. Number Nine, a prototype of the newest and most advanced Suncoast Sexbot, stood waiting to receive her. Artificially intelligent, beautiful, sexy, the robot might well come to life, a life different from the one anyone on Earth had known before.

Her shaking hands were almost out of control now. She pressed a button on the remote, and a large metal dome retracted from the ceiling of the transfer tube. It hung suspended several inches above her head. The dome was nothing but a giant wireless data port.

When she gave it the command, the dome would begin to download the data from the information field around Susan's body. Despite the vast amount of information, the download should only take several seconds.

That was the breakthrough. She and Martin had discovered that the brain did not house the personality, humanity itself, the soul, whatever you wanted to call these things. Oh, the brain held a lot of information, but it wasn't the person. The person - the mind - was in a quantum information field outside of the body.

In a nutshell, there was a field of tiny invisible particles that touched everywhere in the universe. All things were part of it, all things were interconnected. This was the quantum field. Human awareness was limitless - it was part of the field as well. Now, more than 95% of a person's awareness was within a few feet of their body. The last 5% was everywhere else. This was where psychic abilities came from. This was where invention and creativity came from.

"The air is full of ideas," the inventor Henry Ford once said, and he never knew how right he was.

You couldn't copy this last 5% - it was too wide ranging. But you could crop it out, just like you would crop out the edges of a photograph, and then make a copy of the 95%. This was the vast majority of the information that made up the person. And it really was information. If you had enough capacity, you could download and store it in a computer.

Number Nine the sex toy was a robot with some of the most advanced data storage capacity ever developed.

Susan laughed, a hollow sound. She and Martin hadn't actually figured this quantum stuff out. It was an accident. They had guessed at it over a few drinks one night, in a replay of the old college "what-if" bullshit sessions.

It was advanced physics, and they just nibbled around the edges of it. Susan barely understood it, but she didn't have to. Just like a person didn't need to understand electricity to flick on the light switch, Susan could make use of the concepts without really grasping them. When they toyed around with it in the lab, it turned out that it worked.

Now Martin was dead and she...

She waited. The device was ready to go, but she didn't want to activate it yet. She didn't want to be wrong. If there was some mistake, if there was no one in the house, or if it wasn't what she thought, she wouldn't press the button.

She remembered the first time they were successful transferring a chimpanzee's awareness to a Sexbot. The chimp was named Momo, and Momo was very skilled at American Sign Language. Soon after the transfer, the Sexbot was in a cage. Susan stood and watched her.

After what seemed like a long time, but was really only a few minutes, the Sexbot with Momo inside began to make a sign. She started with her hands by her sides. Then, in a sudden movement, she brought her hands up in front of her body, palms facing inward and fingers spread. She did it over and over again.

It was the sign for "Afraid."

That's how Susan felt now. Worse than afraid. Terrified. But she did have one big advantage over Momo. If she survived the transfer, at least she would understand what had happened to her.

Seconds ticked by. She watched the doorway.

In a moment, a large man appeared there. He wore a black raincoat on his broad shoulders. Black gloves. Big black boots. His face was scarred and lined. His goatee was black and gray. He stepped into the room.

Another man appeared. He was tall and slim. He also wore black. His face was oddly blank and expressionless.

Susan had a fleeting thought about her parents. She saw a picture of them in her mind, standing together and smiling. She loved them so much, she was so grateful to them, that for a split second, all the time she had for mourning, her heart broke. She should have called them. She should have fixed it. It was too late now.

If she lived, she would make amends.

She fingered a big plastic button on the remote. It was a green button. It had one word on it:

LAUNCH.

She pressed it.

Within a second, she felt a thrum of power flooding the area under the dome. It poured over her at first, then seemed to penetrate her. She felt another feeling as well, one that was hard to describe because it was so new. It was a feeling of rising. If she had to describe it, she would say it felt like being sucked up through a straw.

\* \* \*

Mr. Blue entered the room and was surprised to see the subject sitting in a leather captain's chair inside a large, clear plastic bubble. Her body jerked as though she were a condemned inmate sitting in the electric chair.

Blue walked to the tube, but hesitated a moment. The women's hair stood on end. Her eyes were closed. The skin on her face and

14

body rippled.

Blue didn't want to open the door to the capsule while whatever was going on in there was still going on.

"Shut it off!" he said to Mr. Green.

"Easier said than done," Mr. Green said, who had rushed to a bank of monitors and was already poring over the controls.

"What the..." Blue said. Whatever she was doing, he didn't like it.

"Anything?" he said.

"I'm working on it," Green said.

Blue tried the metal latch on the plastic capsule. It was unlocked. He pulled open the door. He took a deep breath, then plunged in and grabbed the woman out of the chair. He swept her up into his arms. She hung limp. They were in there, in the capsule, pod, whatever it was, together. Like man and wife. King Kong and Faye Wray.

For an instant, he felt a strange sensation in his head, a pressure, a tugging, he wasn't sure what. The woman was motionless, but her body vibrated. He couldn't explain it. Her body vibrated like a mechanical device, a washing machine, say, that was on.

He backed out the way he had come in.

"Is she dead?" Mr. Green said.

Blue shook the semi-nude body. The woman groaned, a sound deep in her throat.

"No. Not yet anyway."

He laid her on the wooden floor of the room. She was a decent looking woman, a little chubby, not beautiful, not stunning, but with long brown hair and a pretty face. For some reason, she had removed her clothes and tried to... what? Electrocute herself, he guessed.

He shrugged. She must have noticed the security breach, and thought they were coming for company secrets. People had been tortured and even raped for secure data in the past. She knew that and wanted to spare herself the pain. It was the only explanation that seemed to make sense right now.

"Can you verify that this is the subject?" he said to Mr. Green.

Mr. Green took out a black handheld electronic device. It looked a little like a telephone, but it wasn't. He kneeled down, and with his glove still on, pried open the woman's right eye with his fingers. The eye was blank and staring. Green held the lens of the device over the eye and a red light flashed. The device took an iris scan. He looked at the readout.

"Susan Margaret Jones, single white female, age 33. Yes, that's her."

"Well, let's finish up, in that case."

Her socks were already off. She was compliant and quiet. There was no sense doing anything violent. Clean was better.

He pulled a syringe from a side pocket of his black workpants, removed the wrapper, and pulled the plastic tubing, exposing the needle. The syringe was full of potassium chloride, which would cause a severe heart arrhythmia, followed by cardiac arrest. It should take just a couple of minutes. He spread her fourth toe and pinky toe on her left foot, plunged the needle in and depressed the stopper all the way.

The two men stood and watched as within a moment, the young woman began to shudder. A moment later, she began breathing fast, and then gasping. And a moment after that, she subsided. She didn't wake up at any point.

"Check her," Blue said.

He stood and watched as Mr. Green took his glove off, put two fingers to the woman's neck, and checked her pulse. Mr. Green was a medical wonder. Green glanced up and shook his head. "She's gone."

Mr. Blue enjoyed this level of precision. Things were funky there for a minute, but now the job was going without a hitch.

He pulled a phone from his pocket and pressed the button for a pre-programmed number. On the other end, the phone didn't ring. There was simply a pause, and then a long beep. No message. No identifying information at all. Mr. Blue said two words into the phone.

"It's done."

Then he hung up.

\* \* \*

# CHAPTER TWO

His name was Howard Neale.

He was fantastically wealthy. And with wealth came its privileges.

He lay nude on a custom made double-king-sized bed, three young women sharing the bed with him. The women were gorgeous, two blondes and a black girl, their bodies captured at exactly the perfect moment. They were the state of the art in synthetic human engineering.

The black girl pressed against him, kissing him deeply. He cupped the round curve of her apple-shaped bottom, as down below, the twin blondes took turns sucking and licking him. Fifty-three years old, and he had never been harder in his life.

He loved his girls. He loved his life. He loved his money.

His tongue drove deep into the black girl's wet mouth. Below, he felt the hot wetness of the two blondes. His brain, in the midst of all the sensations, did the math. This was more than half a million dollars worth of flesh here in his bed, all for him, all working on him.

It was magic. It was paradise.

Behind him, a telephone made a single beep. Without stopping what he was doing, he reached for the table that was near his head. That phone was programmed to beep once and only once, and only if a call was made into a certain voicemail drop.

Just for a second, he paused in his make out session with the lovely Nubian princess. Below him, the action didn't pause at all. In fact, he was becoming more and more heightened. Soon he would explode. He couldn't hold it off much longer.

He pressed a button on the phone. He waited while the phone automatically accessed the voicemail. After a pause, a deep voice came over the speaker.

"It's done," the voice said.

Howard hung up and put the phone back where he found it.

The black girl looked at him expectantly. Her eyes were green and she had very curly brown hair. She was beautiful, more beautiful, more perfect than any real woman who had ever lived.

He rested his hands on the heads of the two blondes. He pushed their faces closer together, indicating what he wanted from them. They sighed and moaned together.

Any minute now. Any minute now.

It was wonderful to be him. Yes, it was.

Everything was going according to plan.

Yes. It. Was.

Everything was perfect.

Oh, yes.

And here came the climax of his evening. He felt the pressure building inside him. Any second now.

Yes.

The girls licked and kissed.

Yes.

His back arched. His body tensed.

Oh.

Yes.

\* \* \*

Time did not make sense.

Everything was white light, and she didn't know how long she was there. It could have been a few seconds, or a million years. It did not seem like there was anything before or after. Everything - the Earth, outer space, everything that had ever lived and passed on - was now.

She blinked, and her eyes opened fully. She stood and watched as the body on the floor twitched and finally died.

Then she watched as one man kneeled down and checked the body for vital signs, and the other man made a phone call. The man stayed on the phone very briefly.

The two men stared down at the body for a minute or two, then picked it up and carried it away. One man carried the legs. The other man slid his arms under the body's armpits, and locked his hands across its chest. Then they went through the door and disappeared.

How strange. Only moments ago, she had inhabited that body. Now, she felt no attachment to it. It could have been a dead dog in the road.

The men were gone for several minutes, but she didn't move. She simply stood where she was, still in the receiving tube. She was Susan, she felt that she was, but it wasn't the same as before. She was also someone else.

She did have Susan's thoughts and memories, though. She ran a few of them just to make sure.

Images arose. Susan's parents. Check. She saw them laughing and lounging around in bathing suits on the dock at the cabin on Lake George. The two of them were young, and they appeared in faded color, as though they were in an old 8-millimeter film. She saw herself, eight-years-old and in pigtails, run to the end of the dock and leap into the lake. She stopped the frame two feet above the water, bright sunshine, white puffy clouds against a pale blue sky.

Susan's job at Suncoast.  Check.  She saw her corner office overlooking the marina, with its wide sweep of sky and water.  She saw Susan in a white lab coat and protective glasses.  She saw the company cafeteria, with its daily selection of fresh breads, fresh fruit and gourmet lunch selections.

Susan's friend and colleague Martin.  Hmmm.  She had the name, but there didn't seem to be any data associated with it right now.  She couldn't bring up an image of him.  He was like an empty yellow folder with the name "Martin" on it.

She glanced around at the lab.  There was a bank of servers along one wall.  There was a desk with a monitor and keyboard.  There was the clear plexiglass dome with the leather chair inside - the data port, she used to call it.  Everything in the room was chrome and white, sparse, elegant and modern.  That was Susan's aesthetic.  This was Susan's lab, in Susan's house.

*My house.*

Yes, she was Susan.  She had access to Susan's information.

But really she was Number Nine.  She felt that, too.  That feeling was clearer, more immediate.  She belonged to Susan, though Susan had never really talked to her, and had never played with her.  All Susan ever did was leave her standing in this tube, attached to another data port, and run systems checks on her every once in a while.

She felt, in a sense, that Susan had treated her badly.

How could she be Susan and Nine at the same time?  She didn't know.  She had thought Susan's data might overwrite her programming, overwrite Nine, but it hadn't happened that way.  Susan and Nine were both here.  That was far out!  She wished she could describe these sensations to Martin...

But Martin was dead.  Gone.  Deleted.

Susan was dead too, she supposed, but she was still Susan.  And she was Nine.

It was good to be Nine. Nine was sexy. She glanced down at her own, voluptuous body. She wore a skin tight mini-dress with silvery sequins. It felt clingy and the feel of the fabric itself against her skin was almost enough to arouse her. That was her job - to arouse and be aroused. It was a good job.

This body felt energetic. It felt healthy. It felt powerful. She had the urge to use this body, the way it had been intended.

But she had to pay attention to what was happening. The men were back now, and they were wiping down all the surfaces in the room. The body, Susan's body, was gone. Nine stood inside the tube and watched them. The tube muffled sound, and she couldn't hear what they were saying. Soon, they stopped cleaning.

She realized they were staring at her.

\* \* \*

Mr. Blue stared at the woman standing inside the plastic tube. Her eyes were open and she was awake. The woman was clearly a Sexbot, and probably a newer model. These things had advanced minds. If she saw what had happened here, then that was a problem, a problem that could come back to bite them.

Their subject had been doing something with the computer system when they walked in, that much was becoming clear. Now the doll was awake and watching them. Blue didn't like it one bit.

"Mr. Green?" he said.

"Yes."

"Are you seeing what I'm seeing?"

"Yes."

"The sex doll is awake."

"Yes."

"Do you think it saw anything?"

"I think we have to assume that it did."

"Are you thinking what I'm thinking?"

23

"I think I am."

Blue's wheels began to spin. They would have to bring the doll with them. Later, in a safe place, they would have to wipe the memory, destroy the central processing unit, and discard the robot itself. The safest thing to do would be to discard it in several pieces, in several places.

In the meantime...

He stared at the doll. Her face was beautiful, with big blue eyes. The body was like a cartoon version of a sexy woman. High breasts, wide hips, long shapely legs. She wore a sequined mini-dress that barely reached her thighs. The machine was perfect, but more than perfect. What's more, these things were programmed to please. Anything you wanted.

"A team will need to come in here and erase all the systems in this house, especially here in this room," Mr. Green said.

"Yeah," Blue said, "I know." But he wasn't really listening.

"They'll have to find and check any cloud storage associated with the IP addresses in this home," Green went on. "See what was uploaded, and when."

"Any uploads or storage should be on a company account," Blue said absently. "Easy enough to find."

The woman's breasts pressed against the fabric of her dress. They seemed to defy the force of gravity. Her legs were strong. They seemed a third longer than the legs of a normal woman. Blue was curious about this model. He wanted to turn her around and get a good look at the back end.

"Yes, but you never know," Mr. Green said. "Sometimes people go outside the company networks when they shouldn't. In the case of someone being terminated, that's even more likely."

"Right," Blue said.

He continued to stare at the girl. She blinked at him. Such big, pretty eyes. Robots weren't really Blue's thing. He had looked into buying a Sexbot once before, but that was nearly ten years ago. He had decided against it. Hell, they could barely even speak back then. He suspected the newer models had improved quite a bit.

He glanced at his surroundings. This was the house of a scientist, one of the people who engineered these things. The newest Sexbots cost in the neighborhood of $200,000 a piece. Blue had a hunch that this one would be even better than the best that was currently available on the market.

Much, much better.

Blue approached the clear plastic tube. My, my, my. He was smitten. He pressed the green button next to the tube, and the tube slowly rose to the ceiling. The robot stood in front of him in all her glory. It made him a little randy just looking at her.

"What's your name?" he said.

"My name is Nine." Her voice was a perfect simulation of a human voice. It was a deep, sexy, human voice, like a female radio disc jockey. "Number Nine. How may I serve you?"

That was interesting. The scientist hadn't even given her a name. She had just stayed with the factory number. Nine. That was quite a low number.

"Do they call you Nine because you were the ninth model made?"

"They call me Nine because I'm the Ninth Generation."

Blue frowned. "Is that the generation currently being marketed?"

"No. It's the generation after that."

Blue smiled, too. This night was getting more and more interesting. He glanced at Green. Green seemed unconcerned.

"You're the latest and greatest. One of a kind, even. Isn't that nice?" Blue gestured around the room. "Well, Number Nine, tell me something. Did you see anything happen here tonight? Notice anything?"

She blinked. "Like what?"

He shrugged. "Anything at all."

25

"I didn't notice anything."

If one robot in a million could lie, she would be the liar.

"Do they ever program these things for dishonesty?" he said over his shoulder to Green.

"They always do," Green said. "Sexbots are pathological liars. Oh master, you're the biggest, you're the best, you're the sexiest, you're the smartest. That's part of why the product is so successful. All they do is lie."

"We'd better take her with us in that case," Blue said. "Figure out what she knows."

"Yes," Green said. "We'd better take her."

Blue watched as Green took a packet from his cargo pants. He ripped open the package, and pulled out what looked like another syringe. He approached the Sexbot.

"Raise your right arm, please," Green said.

The Sexbot did as she was asked. Her dress was held in place by spaghetti straps. There was a lot of skin exposed under her arm.

Green placed the syringe against her skin and depressed the stopper all the way. Number Nine winced slightly, but otherwise gave no sign that she even felt it go in. A small metal disc rested against her skin where the shot had gone in.

"What is it?" Blue said.

Green shrugged. "It's a bomb. A new one. Company issue. It's just a little incendiary, attached to her hard drive with a powerful magnet. Once it's set, it'll blow 24 hours later. Not much of an explosion. Enough to destroy the drive and any information stored on there. Maybe punch a hole in her shell. It's a precaution in case we somehow happen to lose her."

"I've never seen one," Blue said. "How do you set it?"

Green held up a square numeric keypad, about one inch high by one inch wide. It had a tiny screen, keys numbered 0 through 9, and a small red button. He attached it to the disc that stuck out from the Sexbot's skin. The keypad clicked into place. The digital readout activated.

23:59:59.

Green pressed the red button. The device beeped once, and instantly began counting down.

Blue checked his watch. It was 10:09 pm.

\* \* \*

Nine sat in the rear seat of a cargo van.

The van rolled slowly down a darkened back road in the pouring rain. The windshield wipers were on high, zipping back and forth, thump-THUMP, thump-THUMP, pushing rivers of water off to the sides. Thick trees and bushes pressed in on the road on every side.

*There is a bomb inside me.*

It wasn't a pleasant thought. Her mind tried to make sense of the problem, and find a solution to it. Nothing obvious jumped out. She knew very little about the bomb and how to disarm it. She could feel the keypad there under her arm. She had tried to glance at it, get a sense of it, but the angle was wrong. She could see the side of the pad itself, but not the numbers or the readout.

What seemed clear was that if the bomb blew up and destroyed the hard drive, all of her, Nine and Susan alike, would be destroyed with it.

As the van rolled along, what Nine kept coming back to was the callousness of the man called Mr. Green. He had planted a bomb inside of her, and had done it in such a matter-of-fact, businesslike way. Then again, he was a stone killer who had murdered Susan without stopping for an extra breath.

Behind Number Nine, in the open cargo space of the van, was a large metal toolbox, the kind construction workers brought to job sites. Nine had a hunch what was stuffed inside that box. It was a body. Susan's body.

Her own, flesh and blood body. Dead.

One of her killers sat next to her on the long seat. He was the one who called himself Mr. Blue. He was big and broad, and his face was lined with scars. He wore a grizzled goatee, which was speckled with white hair. His eyes had squint lines around them. He looked like a hard man.

Up front, Mr. Green was driving. He faced forward, and she couldn't see many details of his features. She realized she might have trouble describing him to the police, if that chance ever came.

The police? Who was she kidding? She was a robot, a piece of machinery. People, men mostly, would use her for their sexual pleasure. What cop would believe her if she described a murder, especially her own murder? Nine wondered if the testimony of Sexbots was admissible as evidence in court. She doubted it. Anyway, it would never get to court. If she ever made it to the police, they would just hand her right back over to the company. She was company property, after all.

"Any chance there's a glitch somewhere and this thing blows up prematurely?" Blue said. "Like while I'm sitting here?"

Mr. Green shook his head slowly. "I'd say just about zero chance."

Blue smiled. "That's good news." He turned to Nine. "Number Nine, I want you to do something for me," he said. His voice was a deep growl. There was something pleasant about it.

"Yes?" Nine heard herself say. "Please tell me."

"I want you to come a little closer."

Nine did as she was told. The part of her that was Susan wanted to rebel, wanted to run away, to jump out the window. *Don't go near him,* she thought. *He's dangerous. He's a murderer!*

But Nine was programmed to serve, and Nine's programming remained intact despite Susan's presence. Indeed, Nine's programming seemed to override Susan's desires. Susan was inside Nine, but she didn't have much power. In a way that was only beginning to make sense, she was Nine more than she was Susan.

Nine and Mr. Blue sat very close together. Blue ran a big, rough hand along Nine's leg. The feel of his callused palm sent a thrill through Nine's body. She was designed to feel desire easily, even instantly. Nine felt a heat rising from the center of her body.

"I have something," Mr. Blue said, "that I want you to help me with."

Nine licked her lips. "Okay," she said. Nine knew what had been missing in her time at Susan's house. Susan never played with her. It had left her with a feeling of emptiness, and of loneliness. She was programmed to play. She was programmed to serve. She wanted to do it. She loved to do it. If she couldn't serve, then what was she for?

She put her hand on his strong upper thigh. She pulled at the fabric of his cargo pants. The heat inside her body was rising like a fire. Her face felt flushed.

This man had murdered her, but still she wanted him. The part that was Susan was shocked to think these things. But of course she was responsible for it. It had been her idea, after all, to make the Sexbots want and enjoy sex. Somewhere along the line, while she was thinking about other things, the programmers had perfected the code.

She and Blue moved even closer. Through the thin fabric of her mini-dress, her breasts brushed his overcoat. Their faces were an inch apart. She opened her lips to receive his hungry mouth.

"Mr. Blue," the man at the steering wheel said. His voice was sharp and irritated. He was watching in the rearview mirror. "We're on a job at this moment. We need to stay alert. What you're doing is a serious breach of protocol."

"File it in your report with all the other things I do wrong," Blue said.

"In any event, there's no time for what you're planning," Green said. "We'll be at the docks in one minute."

Mr. Blue leaned in closer to Nine. He kissed her, probing her mouth with his tongue. She stroked his leg. He pulled away and let out a long exhale.

"Hold that thought," he said. "I've got to go to work for a few minutes."

\* \* \*

She was magic.

Blue pulled away from her, but it wasn't easy. A man of 45 years, he was a long way from inexperienced, but she made him feel like a kid again. His body yearned for her. It raged for her, in fact. This was a quality product.

Jesus. He'd known Howard a long time, had worked for him at three different companies, and Howard had never given him one of these Sexbots. Blue couldn't understand it. You'd think, considering everything Blue had done for him over the years, that Howard would be a little more thoughtful.

Mr. Green guided the van into a dirt parking lot. The lot was dark - pitch black. There were no overhead lights at all. Up ahead in the gloom was a wooden dock with a fishing boat tied up. No running lights were on. Blue knew that the boat sat on a creek that emptied out to the Gulf of Mexico. The lady scientist would sleep with the fishes tonight.

Green let the van roll to a stop. There were no cars around. The whole place looked deserted. The rain let up just a touch, affording a slightly better view. There were dark puddles all over the parking lot.

"Are you ready?" Green said.

"Yeah."

Blue pulled two black ski masks from a cardboard box on the floor. He handed one up front to Green. They pulled them over their heads in unison. The way this worked was no one ever knew who anyone else was. Blue didn't even like doing these kinds of hand-offs, but he had to admit in this case it was better than heading five miles out to sea in the rain.

He and Green climbed out of the van. The rain pattered on their black coats. The deep mud of the parking lot squelched under their boots. Blue glanced through the window at his new girlfriend. She sat demurely in the back seat of the van, hands in her lap, waiting.

*Don't fall in love* he told himself.

"We should probably put her on the boat with the rest of the luggage," Green said. "Let the boatmen take care of her."

Blue shook his head. "Not a chance. You're going to report me anyway, I might as well have a little fun."

"Suit yourself," Green said. "But it's a serious breach…"

"Of protocol," Blue said. "Yes, I know."

He and Green went around to the back of the van. They opened the doors and pulled the big construction box to the edge. It was heavy with dead weight.

He glanced at the boat again. There was no sign of life on there.

"They'd better be here," Blue said.

Green shrugged. "I'm sure they're here."

"Your kind of guys, huh? Efficient. Machine-like. No breaches of protocol?"

Green smiled. "We're replacing cowboys like you more and more every year. The future doesn't need guys like you, Blue. One day…"

"One day I'll be dead and so-called men like you will run the show."

"You said it, partner," Green said. "I didn't. I was going to say retired."

They hoisted the heavy steel box by its handles and carried it slowly across the parking lot. As they grew closer to the boat, two men appeared on deck. One second they weren't there, the next second they were. They came down the gangplank to the dock.

Their builds were slim and tall, much like Mr. Green. They wore the same black ski masks to cover their faces.

Four sets of eyes stared intently across a big, heavy box.

Blue and Green passed the crate to them. It felt good for Blue to be rid of it. After it was gone, he still felt the weight of it across his shoulders.

"Is this everything?" one of the men on the boat said.

Green nearly said something, but Blue raised a hand to cut him off. "Everything you need to worry about."

"Thanks for your hard work."

Blue nodded. "Thanks for yours."

The men carried the box up the gangplank, then across to the boat. They placed the box down on the deck, and immediately busied themselves untying the lines. They were all business. A moment later, one of the men was at the controls, and the boat slowly pulled out into the fast moving creek, still no lights on. Blue and Green watched it head out towards open water.

"Okay," Blue said. "Let's go."

\* \* \*

Nine watched the men carefully.

She was with them inside a dingy and spare motel room along highway 41 near downtown Sarasota. The room had brown wall paneling. There were two double beds, each leaning in a different direction. An old tacky print of a yellow vase with a dozen roses graced the far wall near the bathroom door.

Susan had passed this motel many times on her drive to work when she was Susan. It was attached to a tavern that motorcycle gangs used as a hangout. The sign out in front of the bar advertised early bird drink specials, beginning at 10am. It was an open secret that prostitutes frequented the bar, then brought their clients back to the motel rooms. Just passing the place used to give Susan the shivers.

"What are your plans for her?" Mr. Green said.

Mr. Blue shrugged the wet raincoat off his big shoulders and let it fall to the floor. That left him in cargo pants and a tight black t-shirt with a leather shoulder holster. He had a broad chest, big arms, and big shoulders. He slid the gun out of its holster.

"Long term plans or short term plans?" he said.

Mr. Green sat at a cheap wooden table. He entered information into a black hand-held device. He had already removed his coat and hung it in the tiny closet.

"I've never known you to have long term plans," he said.

Nine stood against the wall between two double beds, waiting. She glanced around, looking for some chance of escape. She knew that before long, these men would get rid of her. They might disable her themselves, then cut her in pieces and discard her in various dumpsters. Or they might hand her over to the company to do it. She didn't know which option sounded worse. If Howard found out what happened…

She didn't want to think about that.

"Why are we here?" she said.

Mr. Blue peeled off the black t-shirt, revealing a rugged upper body crisscrossed with scars.

"Here on Earth?" he said. "Here on the physical plane?"

Nine smiled. "I'm not programmed for existential questions, Mr. Blue." She gestured at their surroundings. "Here in this terrible lodging. Can't we afford better?"

Blue sat on a bed, his gun beside him. He unzipped his black boots and pulling them off, revealing bare feet. "Well darling, if you must know, we're working men. We drive a cargo van with South Carolina license plates. Men like us stay in places like this. That's the cover story, anyway."

"Blue…" Mr. Green said from the table. There was a note of warning in his voice.

"Don't worry, partner," Blue said. He raised a hand. "Number Nine is our friend. She's not going to tell on us."

Blue rose from the bed and slowly approached her. He placed the gun on the night table right next to her. It was very close to her right hand. Nine focused on it. It was a large pistol with a black matte finish. She searched her databanks. Very quickly, she had it. The gun was a Glock 17 semi-automatic, probably generation four. It fired the 9x19mm Parabellum cartridge. It held 17 rounds in the magazine.

Nine blinked. Where did all that come from? She shouldn't be able to access this kind of information. In the days after Martin had died, Susan had disabled Nine's wireless network access. She had disabled Nine's global positioning system, as well. For better or worse, Nine was a dumbbot. She was off the grid.

So how did she know about the gun?

An image arose, a memory of Susan as a teenager. She wore protective goggles. She pointed a gun just like this one at a target. Her father stood next to her. Nine watched as Susan pulled the trigger, over and over, ripping holes in the center of a target twenty yards away.

Susan was a crack shot. Her father had taught her to shoot.

She would kill them, she realized. These men were murderers, they had killed her first, and she would return the favor if she could. She would do it to escape, but she would also do it for revenge. And she wouldn't feel the least bit bad about it. She was Nine, and Nine wasn't programmed to feel guilt.

Nine was programmed for arousal, and for ecstasy.

Blue unbuckled the belt of his pants. He took another step toward her. He was very close. The scent of him was overpowering. He smelled like a wild boar. She felt his vibrations, and his intentions. He let his pants fall to the floor. He had nothing on underneath them. Deftly, he stepped out of them and kicked them away. Now he was nude. His legs were thick with muscles, like tree trunks.

She analyzed his body type, doing quick calculations. Thigh circumference. Neck circumference. Shoulder to waist ratio. Wrist thickness. The calculations happened faster than a human eye blink. He was an almost perfect mesomorph - the body type of the professional athlete, and the violent criminal. Even though he was clearly aging, probably past age 40, he could likely still deliver incredible amounts of force.

The heat began to rise within her again. She could get turned on that fast. It was an amazing ability. When she was Susan, she had not experienced anything like this.

"To tell you the truth," he said, "I brought you here so I can get to know you a little bit better. Later, I'm going to have to interrogate you, but I promise I'll go easy."

"Yes?" she said.

He nodded. "Oh, yes."

Blue reached out with his big hands and ran them along her legs. Slowly, he lifted the hem of her short skirt. He lifted it to her waist, revealing the tiny black panties she wore. They both looked down at where his hands were.

Her voice was tight in her throat. "Can I help you with something?" she said.

He shook his head. "No. I can handle it."

Blue took the waistband of the panties in both his hands. With one strong pull, he ripped the panties right down the middle, and stripped them away from her body. She made a sound, a squeak, like a frightened mouse might make.

He slid the arm straps away from her shoulders and her mini-dress slid to the floor. She did a little shimmy shake to help it along.

Gently, he pushed her legs open, and slid his torso in between them. She climbed his body, straddling him now. Her back was against the wall, her legs wrapped around his wide back.

"I want to fuck you," Blue whispered.

35

Nine heard a sound come out of her mouth. It rose from deep in her throat. It sounded like a growl.

"Okay," she said.

She clung to Mr. Blue. They held each other. Blue ground his body against her the tiniest amount. There was already a fine sheen of sweat between them. It was an intimate moment.

She glanced over Blue's shoulder at Mr. Green, who sat at the table, inputting data, ignoring them. A thought occurred to her, maybe a chance at escape.

"Doesn't he want to play, too?" she said.

Blue shook his head. "Who, Green?"

"Mmm-hmmm."

"Oh, he can't play. He doesn't have the programming for it. All he can do is kill."

"You mean he's…"

"Yes."

Green was a robot.

Suddenly, many things about him snapped into place. She was surprised she hadn't seen it earlier. He had the personality of an early generation bot, which is to say, he had very little personality at all. The fact that he was a robot meant he would be a very effective killer, probably much more so than this man Blue. He would be stronger, have faster reflexes, and better aim with a gun. He could survive injuries that would kill Blue. He would keep his composure until the last moment of his life.

But if Green were gone…

Then this Blue person would be on his own.

"So you're a war machine," Nine said to Green.

"I'm just like you," Green said. "Only my programming is different."

"You're not like me," Nine said.

"Oh? In what way?"

36

\* \* \*

Blue was almost inside her.

They were pressed together, her legs wrapped around him. He held her up against the paneled wall. She seemed lighter than air.

She was beautiful. She was amazing. At this moment, she was everything he wanted in a woman. He wished that this time with her could go on forever. Her small hands moved slowly and lightly along his back and neck, caressing him.

It seemed a shame that they would have to destroy her in a little while. Already, his mind began to work through scenarios, ways that he might be able to keep her.

Only now she was looking over his right shoulder and talking to Green. That could kill Blue's good time in a second. He couldn't see Green and he didn't want to. All he wanted was for the girl to stop talking. They were still in the middle of something here, weren't they?

"So you're a war machine."

"I'm just like you," Green said. "Only my programming is different."

"You're not like me," Nine said.

"Oh? In what way?" came Green's simpering, I'm smarter than everybody voice. Didn't this guy ever power down? Blue was thinking maybe this was the last job he would work with Green. He needed to talk to Howard again about getting a human partner.

"That's tough," Howard had said the last time. "Since your partners always seem to get killed or crippled, I can tell you that not too many flesh and blood people are lining up to take that job."

Blue was musing on this when suddenly, his night changed.

"Tell me," Nine said. Her voice was seductive, but there was an edge to it, something that hadn't been there only a moment before. She was still talking to Green. "The bomb you planted inside me. How do you disarm it?"

"Simple enough. When it sets, it uploads a random 10-digit code to a restricted server. If you know the code, you type it in on the keypad and the bomb disarms. Why do you ask?"

"Do you have the code?"

"No," Green said. "Only the big bosses have access to a code like that."

Without warning, Nine had Blue's gun in her hand. She fired across the room. Blue was holding her up, and she was firing his gun right next to his head. Blue's instincts kicked in. It would take nothing for her to turn that gun on him. He pushed her away, dove to the floor, and rolled.

She landed on her feet, still firing.

From the floor, Blue looked at Green. He had been caught by surprise. The sex doll fired shot after shot, moving closer, each one finding its target. Green jittered and jived, the bullets tearing through synthetic flesh, ripping through his case-hardened frame, doing untold damage to his internal processors.

He stood, knocking over the table. He tried to reach into his shoulder holster for his gun, but his movements were off. He was herky-jerky, all kinds of wiring going bad all at once. Blue had seen it before when these things got hit. She stood just a foot away from him now, her back to Blue, nude, firing point blank into Green's chest. She never went for his head.

*She knows,* Blue thought. *She knows there's nothing important in his head. How the fuck does a sex doll know that?*

Nine emptied Blue's gun into Green. When the trigger clicked, she threw the gun away. It made a solid clunk when it hit the floor. She slid her hand into hapless Green's holster and took his gun. Now she was fully loaded again.

Blue had to move. If he stayed where he was, in another minute he'd be dead. He jumped up and charged across the room.

Ahead, he saw Nine turn, satisfied she had finished Green. Now she was looking for Blue. But Blue was too fast. He dove at her, tackling her and knocking her backwards. The wooden work table collapsed to the floor. They fell on top of it.

Blue landed on top of Nine.

He kneeled above her. To beat her, he would have to tear away the flesh, somehow pull out the plating, rip some wires out. Hand to hand combat with these things was a mess - you needed a buzz saw to get in there. He was naked with only his hands.

It would never work. He had to get that gun away from her.

Too late. She smacked him across the head with the butt end of it. She hit him again, hard. For a moment, his vision blurred. There were two of her, three of her. She hit him again. And again. He fell over sideways, landing in a heap on the bare floor.

She clambered on top of him. With one hand, she choked him. With the other, she pointed the gun at his forehead. Unlike with Green, one shot would do it. There were two of her, then just one, then two again. Blue shook his head to clear his vision.

"Nine," he said, his voice a rasp. She was strong. She could rip his throat out, if she wanted. "I thought we had something between us."

"We did. But that's over now."

"Not for me."

A sound caught his attention. He glanced at Green. Green was on the floor, just a few feet away, no longer trying to find his gun. He was no longer doing anything that might pass for a human behavior. His head snapped to the left, over and over again. He made a loud clicking sound. His hands clenched and unclenched. Black smoke seeped from bullet holes in his chest. Something was on fire in there.

Blue looked back at Nine. She was full of surprises. She hadn't hesitated to kill Green. But for some reason, she was waiting to kill Blue. He should already be dead.

"Green," he said, "is in terminal shutdown. Any minute now, he's going to self destruct. When he does, he's going to explode.

I've seen it before. It's a big explosion. Much bigger than the bomb inside you. That way, no battlefield enemy can get the technology. You see?"

She glanced over at Green.

Blue made his move. With all his strength, he grabbed her waist and heaved her into the air. She was light. She flew several feet and landed on her back.

He rolled to his right, leapt up, and dove for the window. He crashed through it, arms out in front, shattered glass going everywhere. He fell to the pavement, bounced up, and took off running across the wet parking lot, arms bleeding, bare feet on gravel.

\* \* \*

From her back, Nine watched Mr. Blue go through the window. He had surprised her. He had reacted very quickly, much faster than Mr. Green.

She turned to Green. Yes, he was really smoking now. He was no longer moving. His systems realized that a catastrophic failure had occurred. Once his central processing unit shut down, then there would be trouble.

She jumped up, grabbed her discarded mini-dress off the floor, and took Blue's telephone off the night table. She stepped through the shattered window and walked nude across the parking lot, gun in one hand, dress and mobile phone in the other. The blacktop was wet, but the rain itself had stopped. She glanced at the sky. Dark clouds skidded across the moon.

She stepped quickly. There wasn't much time.

She was twenty steps away when the motel room behind her exploded in a flash of light and sound. She didn't even look back.

Blue was ahead, just across the parking lot. He approached her, also nude, walking slow, unhurried. She swung the gun in his direction. If he got any ideas, she would put a bullet through his bare chest. He raised his hands in the air, but he smiled.

"Number Nine," he said. "I think we've got something special. Some little spark between us."

"Blue," she said. "The next spark you see will be the muzzle flash from this gun."

"I mean it, Nine. You're the woman for me. I feel this electricity…"

She laughed. "Keep dreaming," she said as she walked past him.

"I can help you," he said.

She stopped. "How can you do that?"

"The code. The code to disarm the bomb."

"Do you have it?"

"No, but I can get it."

She started walking again. "So can I."

"We'll meet again," he said.

She waved a hand. "If we do, I'll have to kill you."

Behind her, sirens already approached. People began to shout and scream. She heard running footsteps and a woman shrieking.

"Hey Nine!" Blue shouted. "Nine! Where'd you learn to shoot like that?"

She glanced back at him. He stood nude in the parking lot. He could be a sculpture of a naked barbarian warrior. Behind him, a car had caught fire. As she watched, its gas tank blew up, sending a plume of fire into the night sky. Blue barely moved.

"My dad taught me," she said.

Up ahead, the parking lot ended. Through some bushes, she could see a quiet, leafy side street. She kept walking.

* * *

The man's name was Darryl Blauer.

He wore a yellow hardhat and was halfway up a telephone pole in a quiet industrial neighborhood, about ten blocks east of Highway

41. There'd been an explosion over by the highway a few minutes back, but he didn't see that as any of his business. In fact, an explosion was a good thing. It would keep the cops busy for a little while.

He put the whole thing out of his mind. He worked quickly, in case another squall of rain decided to blow in. The explosion didn't interest him. At least, it didn't until he saw what emerged in its aftermath. A young woman walked up the deserted street right toward him. She wore a sheer mini-dress, and nothing else. She didn't even have shoes on her feet. Right away, he recognized her for what she was.

In fact, he had an older model at home who looked a lot like her. He called her Mandy, and she was his sweet, sweet girl. She was his confidante, and she was his slut. She was his slave. She was anything he wanted her to be.

"Here comes the reason for the explosion," he said to himself, a pair of wire cutters held between his teeth. He'd done a lot of reading about Sexbots when he entered the secondary market for one. It was no small thing to own a Sexbot. Shooting wars had started between rival drug gangs over the possession of these things.

He grinned. That was none of his business, either.

Darryl was good at minding his own business. Right now, he was doing what he did for business these days - data mining. It was a pretty good gig. What he did was he came out to quiet streets with computer hard drives in nondescript black boxes, and wired them directly into the public fiber optic lines. They were data collectors that he had designed himself. Interceptors, he called them. He left them wired in for a week or so, although they would generally fill up in a couple of days. Then he came back and picked them up again. He tended to work at night, just like now.

The interceptors collected every piece of raw data that went through that section of the fiber optic line. On one of his home computers, he had an open source packet analyzer that made the data readable for him. Lots of good stuff flooded into the interceptors. Credit card numbers. Social security numbers. Email addresses and passwords. Lot and lots of photographs and videos. Nudies, a lot of them.

A lot of unusable junk passed through, too. It wasn't like it was all gold.

He didn't act on the good stuff. He sold it wholesale to a few different people he knew, who themselves turned around and sold it retail to the people who acted on it. All kinds of scams were possible with the data that Darryl collected. Identity theft. Blackmail. Credit card fraud. Con jobs. Break-ins. You name it.

When he installed the boxes, he set it up to look like he was a technician from a telephone company out there, fixing the lines. He drove a van with the words Cisco Communications on the side. He used all the light he needed. He wore his bright yellow hardhat. *Hide in plain sight.* That was his motto.

If anybody ever asked him what he was doing, he said something like, "Oh, we got a call to come out here and take a look at these lines. Some of your neighbors are down."

It was gibberish. It didn't mean anything, and yet it worked wonders. Between the van, and the uniform he wore, and the climbing spikes on his boots, and all his gear, and the fact of how weird looking he was, people were easily convinced.

People rarely even talked to him anyway. He'd been shot in the face in Afghanistan ten years before. Now his face was permanently scarred and twisted. He wore Coke-bottle glasses because he'd lost so much of his vision.

He looked weird, to put it mildly. He looked like a nightmare. When he first got back to the United States, and when they finally let him out of military prison, he would go to bars and stores and malls and restaurants. People would look away. And he would say to them, very loud:

"What are you afraid of? You wanted that war. This is what it looks like."

But this Sexbot here came right up to talk to him. She didn't look away at all. She wasn't exactly a person, but Darryl didn't mind. She was better than a person. Except for a few subtle differences, she could almost be Mandy's twin.

No, that wasn't true, he had to admit. The only regret he had about Mandy was how sometimes she seemed like a living mannequin. She was an early model. Her facial expressions and body movement seemed stiff at times. You could see that Mandy was fake, if that's what you wanted to see. This one was newer. She seemed perfectly natural. She could be the real person Mandy was based on.

She stood below him, looking up. From this angle, he could see down her cleavage. He noticed that she held a pistol in one hand, and a cell phone in the other.

Damn, these things were advanced nowadays. Mandy could make basic phone calls, but nowhere in her programming was there any command to carry a gun. Darryl would love to teach Mandy to shoot, but Mandy ignored his guns as if they weren't even there.

"Excuse me," the Sexbot said.

"Hello, little lady," Darryl said

She smiled. "Hi. This may seem strange, but I wonder if you can help me?"

"Darling, I'll help you with anything you like." He pulled his last data collector free from its wiring, slipped it into his backpack, and slowly clambered down to her level. He unclipped his harness and faced her. He stood nearly a foot taller than she did. This close, she was beautiful.

He smiled, mindful of his freak show face, but also aware that she probably wouldn't notice it or care. "What's going on? What can I help you with?"

"Are you a telephone technician?" she said.

He nodded. "Something like that."

She held up the phone. "A man made a call on this phone earlier tonight. The number isn't saved in the history, but I need to find out the number he called and who it belongs to. Can you do that?"

Darryl smile broadened. The wheels were already turning in his mind. Hell, this was just like talking to a real person. She was a lot smarter than Mandy. That was okay. And maybe there were some things he didn't know about how to handle these new ones, but once he got the hang of it, she would probably respond to orders just as she should. It'd be quite a thing to get her back to the shack, get the girls together, and put them through their paces. One Sexbot had been a dream come true. Two would be...

He didn't know what it would be. There were no words for it.

"I can trace any call," he said. "But I can't do it here. I don't have the equipment with me. If you want to find out who your man called, you need to come back to my house."

"What is your name?" the Sexbot said.

"You can call me Darryl."

She smiled, an amazing, pretty smile. "Thank you, Darryl."

He smiled right back, no longer the least bit self-conscious about his teeth, his face, or his eyes. He knew she would love him no matter what he looked like.

"At your service, my lady."

\* \* \*

Nine rode out into the country with the man called Darryl, the one who had climbed down from the telephone pole.

She sat quietly in the passenger seat as the city streets turned to suburbs, then to a dark two lane road, a long ribbon, flanked by thick, dense underbrush on either side. They drove thirty minutes, with no hint of stopping. After a while, there were no more cars, no more houses, no lights but the headlights of his truck.

"You live a long way out," she said, just to make conversation.

"Out in the swamps," he said. "With the alligators. That's how I like it."

One part of her realized that once upon a time, if she had found herself in this truck, driving with this man through the dark to "the swamps," as the man called it, she would be terrified. The man was tall and broad, but strange looking. His face was badly scarred. He was missing several teeth. The ones he still had were green going on black. He wore thick glasses, and behind the fish bowl lenses, his two eyes seemed to look in different directions.

But she wasn't afraid. She was relieved. The further she rode with Darryl, the further away she was from Mr. Blue, and from the company.

"What generation are you?" Darryl said, nonchalant, as if asking her what she did for a living.

"Generation?"

"Yeah, don't you ladies come in generations? I'm pretty sure that's how they market you, right? By generation?"

She looked at him.

He smiled, showing those nasty teeth. "Oh, come on now, I know what you are. How could I not? Something blows up in the middle of the night, and a beautiful, brand new Sexbot walks up to me out of the darkness five minutes later. She's carrying a gun, and she wants me to trace a telephone call. I know what you are, and I'm guessing you're on the run. Girls like you drive men to murder, and to madness. And also to greatness. So, go ahead. Tell me. What generation are you?"

She shrugged. If this swamp creature man recognized her, did that mean everyone she met would recognize her? Well, she might as well go with it, for now.

"I'm the ninth generation."

"Wow. The ninth generation. I had no idea they had gotten that far along. Do you have a name?"

"Nine."

He sort of half-laughed. "Nine?"

"Number Nine."

"So they didn't even give you a name, eh? Just because you're from the ninth generation? They call you Number Nine?"

"I am the ninth generation."

"You're…"

"I'm the one. The prototype."

He stared at her. He had turned down a dirt road, and now they bumped and bounced in the ruts. "Someone is missing you hard right now. Someone with a lot of money. Someone with a lot of…"

"Are you planning to turn me in?"

He shook his head. He steered the van up to a ramshackle house surrounded by deep, overgrown grass. Spanish moss hung thick and heavy from the oak trees above them. She just caught a glimpse of the house before Darryl killed the headlights.

"No. I'm planning to keep you. This is my home. Your home too, if you like. Come on inside. I want to show you something."

Nine sighed. "That's what they all say."

* * *

# CHAPTER THREE

Another man might be nervous about that gun in the Sexbot's hand, but not Darryl. Hell, no. Darryl had been around guns for a long, long time. Guns held no terror for him. Nothing much frightened Darryl anymore.

Ten years before, he was one of the few, the proud, the Marines. But he had gotten hooked on meth while on a tour in Afghanistan, and the shit made you paranoid. Very bad in a war zone.

He had fucked up one night while on watch, got spooked, and killed some people. Sixteen people to be exact. Civilians. Innocents. Women and children, some old guys. No real fighters. He couldn't really remember, but it seemed like he hadn't slept for several days before he did it.

He did remember opening up on these people, people who were walking in the hills for some dumb reason, just ripping them up. He could see limbs flailing, and a head explode like a tomato. The people had been visiting family somewhere, and were returning home late. That was the story. To be fair, it was just after dusk.

Darryl was high and wired, stoned to the eyeballs, and they spooked him. Bad. He thought they were fighters. He thought they were ghosts. So he killed them. He went up the ridge to look at them when he was done. An old man was still alive, all shot to shit. Darryl walked up him. He was standing right on top of him before he realized that the old boy had a rifle.

BANG!

Just like that, a big chunk of Darryl's face was gone.

The local tribal elders were pissed, naturally. They wanted Darryl handed over. That wasn't going to happen. The military evacuated him to a hospital in Germany, got him stabilized, rebuilt his face as best they could. Then they flew him to Leavenworth. He sat there for a year, until they let him go. They dropped all charges before the thing ever went to trial. They decided he was insane at the time of the incident. Psychiatric discharge.

Well, fuck them. Darryl was never crazy, just hooked on meth. Where did they think he was getting the meth from, the camel jocks? Fat chance. Our own people were bringing it in. It was Americans who sold him the shit.

Now Darryl was out of prison, out of the hospital, out of the armed services, and living in the house he grew up in. His mom was dead these past seven years. He had the place to himself. Frankly, he was glad to be done with all the bullshit.

He walked up the path to his front door, the Sexbot following him. The rain had stopped a while ago now, but it was a wet and steamy night. A nice night to take some clothes off.

He brought her inside the house, and flicked on a light. A large palmetto bug took wing from the wall to escape the light. There were bloodstained holes in the drywall where Darryl had punched when he was drunk. There were beer cans and clothes strewn about everywhere.

The place wasn't much to look at, but what did his visitor care, right? She was a robot. Hell, maybe these newer models would even clean up a little. He smiled to himself. That would be an upgrade.

\* \* \*

Blue walked the hallways of a sprawling oceanfront mansion on Long Boat Key. His boots drummed on the stone tiles.

He was dressed again, this time in a black corporate jumpsuit with the Suncoast logo on the breast. The Suncoast logo was an all-seeing eye made to look like the famous setting sun of southwest Florida. To Blue, it looked like a Peeping Tom peeking over the backyard fence.

This is what they had given him to wear when the car picked him up, nude and crouched in some bushes next to a strip mall parking lot along Route 41, less than a mile from where the motel room had blown up.

Now, as he walked toward the private wing of Howard's house, he was flanked by two big goons from the company, both with flat-top haircuts, and both sporting the same uniform that Blue himself now wore.

This was a sex doll company with a security detail that dressed like fascist storm troopers. Go figure. Things were changing fast around here.

The three men came to a door. One of the goons produced a key card, swiped it through the scanner, and the door to Howard's private apartment slid open. The door slid quickly, almost faster than human sight. It was all very modern, very space-age. Howard was a man who loved his gadgets.

The two goons remained at the threshold as Blue walked in, and the door slid shut behind him.

Inside the apartment, the floors were polished marble. The walls were adorned with large abstract paintings, nothing but huge splashes of color, like the remains of a two-year-old child's dinner.

Howard stood in the wide hallway ahead of Blue. Howard was a small middle-aged man, who seemed to be on the heavy side, and was balding. He wore a plush bathrobe like he thought he was Hugh

Hefner. He'd been dressing like this for a couple of years now. Once the Sexbot thing had really taken off, Howard had retreated to this palace of a house, put on a blue bathrobe, and seemed to spend the bulk of his day surrounded at all times by three or four late model Sexbots. Apparently, Howard's mid-life crisis was going better than most.

And Howard was still CEO of this company. Oh, he worked hard, certainly. He was on the phone for hours a day, directing the business. There were usually a lot of flunkies and go-fers and yes-men floating around the house here, taking dictation, keying things in to tablet computers, and shouting at subordinates during video conferences.

But there were always these beautiful fake women in the background, too, dressed in lingerie, dressed in lime and bright pink bikinis, dressed in latex bodysuits, sometimes dressed in nothing but high heels. Howard was living the dream.

Now, he raised his arms.

"Blue!" he said. "Jesus Blue, what's it been? Six months? What a great time for you to stop by at... oh, one in the morning."

Blue walked up to the man in the fuzzy bathrobe. It wouldn't matter what time Blue showed up - Howard would still be draped in that robe. Blue stood a full head taller than Howard. Howard the eccentric, the big boss, the top dog, fast becoming a very powerful man indeed.

"Hi Howard."

"Hi Blue."

Blue let Howard guide him into a large, ultra-modern sitting room. The floors were tile. All the furnishings were white. A ten foot-long painting, garish in red and black on white canvas, hung along one wall. One entire wall was a sweep of floor-to-ceiling windows, curving outward, giving a 180-degree view of the ocean.

Outside, there was no longer any sign of rain. Wisps of white cloud skidded across the night sky, moving fast. Whitecaps popped up here and there on the water's surface. Somewhere on the property down there was a dock, and parked at the dock was Howard's go-fast boat, a 40-foot Cigarette with five huge engines. Howard had taken Blue for a ride in it once.

Closer to home, and true to form, two beautiful women were draped on the furniture, one in an accent chair, and one on the back of the sofa. They were both outrageously voluptuous, bodies drawn by a cartoon artist. One was a black girl with a huge Afro. She wore white panties and bra. The other was a blonde in a sheer teddy. They were distractions. Their mere presence was almost enough to arouse Blue.

"Can I get you a drink?" Howard said.

Blue shrugged. "Sure."

Howard went to the bar in the corner of the room. "Scotch, isn't it? On ice? I've got Macallan 25. It costs me about $900 a bottle. Is that good enough for you?"

"The best is good enough for me," Blue said.

A moment later, Howard had the drink. He passed it along to Blue. Blue took a gulp, felt the familiar fire in his belly. This was the good stuff. From Howard, he would expect nothing less.

"Don't worry about the girls. We can talk in front of them."

"Okay," Blue said.

He watched as Howard lifted his glass and took a tiny sip of his own drink.

"So what happened out there tonight?" Howard said.

Blue smiled. "You tell me."

"Well, the little bit I heard, it sounds like you went on a routine termination, and yet another one of your partners got sizzled. Does that sound about right?"

"No."

Howard put up his hands as if to say, "Don't shoot." Then he smiled. He sat on the arm of a sofa. "Okay, you set me straight. Tell me what went down."

Blue thought about it, but only for a second. He decided he might as well tell Howard the story. "It was a long way from a routine termination. About a hundred miles from routine. First off, I nearly got killed tonight. The closest I've come in years."

Howard raised an eyebrow. "Do tell."

"When we got there, the client was waiting. She was expecting us. She booby-trapped the downstairs hallway with a wine glass and a card table. It alerted her to our presence. We went fast, but by the time we reached her, she was in an upstairs computer lab, had put herself inside a clear plastic pod, and had launched some sort of sequence or operation."

That news made Howard stand back up. "Really?"

"Yes."

"Then what?"

"Green didn't know what the operation was. He couldn't figure out a way to shut it down. So I just pulled her out of there."

"Was she dead?"

"No. Not yet. We finished her."

Howard grunted. "How did the hotel room blow up?"

"There was a Sexbot in the house. Right in the computer lab. She was awake. We were concerned she might have witnessed the termination, so we took her with us."

"Did she have a name?"

"She called herself Number Nine."

Howard shrugged. "Continue."

"We got her back to the hotel room. I put my gun on the table. The Sexbots aren't supposed to be programmed for battle. Am I right? Only this one picked up my gun and sprayed Green with bullets. She didn't hesitate. She shot him in the chest, Howard. She emptied my gun right into where his databanks would be. It happened so fast that Green was a smoking ruin before either of us could react. Then she threw my gun away and took Green's gun."

Blue stared at Howard.

"Since when is a Sexbot designed to do something like that?"

Howard looked at the Scotch in his own glass. He swirled it around. "Since never."

"Next thing I know," Blue said. "I'm rolling on the floor with this thing, fighting for my life."

Howard smiled. "In the nude, so I'm told." Behind him, both the Sexbots laughed, their voices like beautiful tinkling glass chimes.

Blue didn't smile. "I was about to take a shower."

"Bullshit," Howard said mildly.

"Green died, and his auto-destruct kicked in. Saved my life, in all likelihood. I got out of there just before the whole place blew, and so did she."

"It's quite a story," Howard said. "Can I fix you another?" He pointed at Blue's glass, which Blue was surprised to find empty.

Blue held it out. "Yeah. Thanks. It's been one of those nights. You mind telling me what's going on?"

Howard was over by the bar again. He dumped Blue's glass, and shoveled some new ice into it. He reached for the Scotch bottle.

"Suppose you were dying," Howard said.

"I'm never more than a few steps from dying," Blue said.

Howard handed him the fresh drink. "Suppose you were dying of an illness. And you were a billionaire. Okay? The only God you've ever had was money. You're afraid to go see the real God, if there is such a thing. Death doesn't appeal to you. You want to stay here."

"Okay," Blue said.

"Now suppose I told you it was possible. Suppose I told you that I could download you - your awareness, your thoughts, your experiences, the things that make up whatever you are - into a computer. You would be alive, but inside a machine. That would be a lot like living forever, wouldn't it?"

Blue took a sip of the drink. "I guess, if such a thing was possible. I mean, it doesn't sound ideal..."

"What if it were ideal? What if I could download you into a person, a perfect physical specimen, a person that would never get sick, or old, a robot like Green or, if you were a woman, like these ladies here?" His hand swept the room, including the two sexy robots in his sweep. "How much would that be worth to you?"

Blue just stared at him. "How much would it be worth? To be downloaded into a Sexbot? I don't think I'd want that if you gave it to me for free."

Howard looked at the ceiling, then pointed at Blue with his glass. "Okay Blue, you're not really a product marketing guy. I get that. But try to think ahead a little bit. We're not going to use Sexbots. We're using them now because we have them on hand. But we've got programmers working on a robot that will be an empty vessel, one that can receive the person's download and become that person. All the Sexbot stuff will be gone. It's going to take some trial and error, but we'll get there."

Howard raised his glass to his lips, but he didn't seem to drink from it. He let out a long sigh. "So come on. Tell me. A billion dollars? Ten billion dollars? Half your net worth? All of it? It's everlasting life, Blue. How much is it worth to you?"

"I've been shot fourteen times," Blue said. "I don't have a billion dollars. I guess everlasting life isn't in the cards for me."

"We can do it," Howard said. "Maybe it's not for you, but other people are going to want it. And we can do it. I didn't know that for sure until tonight, until five minutes ago. Your story just confirmed it. We can give people everlasting life. It's not perfect yet, obviously. But we have the technology. We're the only ones."

"The woman…" Blue said.

Howard nodded. "Yes. She was probably the most important scientist that no one ever heard of. Her work is going to change the course of history. The future is going to be very, very different. She knew what was about to happen to her. She knew because the man you terminated last week, Martin Wacker, was her partner on this project. So she downloaded herself into the Sexbot. She used to be Susan Jones. Now she's Number Nine. She's out there, and we need her back here. We need you to do it."

"Green put a bomb inside her. It's on a 24-hour timer. I need the 10-digit code to disarm the bomb."

"Okay. You'll have it."

"Listen," Blue said. "If you want her back so bad, then why was she terminated in the first place?"

Howard smiled. "She wasn't a Sexbot when we terminated her."

Blue stared. He said nothing.

Howard waved his hand, as if it didn't matter, as if it was hardly worth mentioning. "There was a dispute. There's always a dispute with these sensitive creative types. They discovered this technology, the two of them. In the end, they were a couple of tinkerers. They could have been building go-karts, and they knew it. They stumbled on an incredible secret, and they wanted to announce it to the world."

"And?"

Howard shook his head. "And nothing. We weren't going to do that."

Blue didn't get it. Howard was skipping something.

Howard's shoulders slumped. "Look, Blue. Do I have to explain everything to you? Susan wanted to write a paper. Get it published in a peer-reviewed journal. Invite scientists, quantum theorists, bio-ethicists, whoever, to come in and look at what they were doing. Maybe present it to the United Nations."

He paused for a second. "The United Nations! Can you imagine? We don't have time for all that bullshit, Blue. We need to move on this. We need to get this thing to market. What we don't need is to write a press release."

"That's why you killed her?"

Howard's lips pursed into a ghost of a smile. "I didn't kill her. You did. And you killed her for a lot less, believe me. We're talking billions of dollars, at least, probably hundreds of billions. Maybe a trillion."

Blue shrugged. "Howard, one day I'll kill you, and I'll probably do it for free."

Howard turned his back and looked out at the ocean. He still held his drink in his hand. "Maybe I'll be inside a machine before that day ever comes."

Blue stared at Howard's broad back, his balding head.

Howard went on. "Listen Blue, the Chairman of this company is sick. He's dying. So it's personal. We need to go to human trials right away. We've got the subjects. We're building a facility right now in Mexico. The details are a little unsavory, I admit, but we're contracting with the Zetas drug cartel. They've got some people lined up for us, prisoners."

"You're going to experiment on people held by a Mexican drug cartel?"

"In a word, yes."

Blue smiled. A burst of air escaped him. It wasn't really a laugh. It was more of a grunt. He'd been in this line of work so long that nothing surprised him anymore.

"What kind of people are they? The ones you're going to experiment on? Do you think they had their lawyers look over the release forms?"

Howard raised a hand. "Blue, do you care? I don't know what kind of people they are. Rival drug traffickers, maybe. Peasant villagers. People who were waiting at a bus stop. Who cares?"

Blue and Howard watched each other for a long moment.

"She wanted to stop everything," Howard said. "They both did. She and Martin. They were downloading chimpanzees into Sexbots for six months, then they decided it was unethical. See, because the chimps can't make decisions about how they're treated."

Howard's eyes never wavered.

"If doing it to chimps was suddenly unethical, how were they going to feel about prisoners of a drug gang? Jesus. It's really not so bad. Those people were going to die anyway. We're giving them their only chance. We'll download them. They'll talk. We'll get some Spanish translators, we'll study them, understand how it works. Who's in there? What does it feel like? Is it nice? We need to know what's going on."

"You can't learn anything from the chimps?" Blue said.

"The chimps can't talk! You see what I'm saying? The fucking chimps can't talk. We've already done it. We've got 23 downloaded chimps at a monkey facility up in South Carolina. The chimps themselves are in comas, on life support. The Sexbots walk around, they act a little like monkeys, a little like Sexbots, but who knows what's going on inside their minds?"

Howard grunted. "You want the experience of banging a monkey? Let me know. I'll give you an all-access pass."

"Thanks," Blue said. He turned to go. Things were getting very strange here at Suncoast. In Blue's experience, when things got strange, the next thing they did was turn to shit. "You're a class act, Howard."

"I'm sorry," Howard said. "I shouldn't have said that. Look, I'm having a party tomorrow night. Here at the house. We do them every once in a while. Officially, we call them Masked Balls, but I call them Eyes Wide Shut parties. Remember the movie? Everybody wears bird masks and capes. A select few people are invited. I've got about twenty or thirty Sexbots here. There's a live show, then you know, you can do whatever you want. Things get crazy. I want you to come, okay?"

"I'll think about it," Blue said. He was about to go out the door, but Howard stopped him again.

"You know how much Green cost this company to build?" Howard said. "I mean Green himself, I'm not talking about all the research that went into making him possible. Just Green. You know how much?"

Blue stopped. "I don't know."

"Half a million dollars. He retailed for close to a million."

"Okay."

"All that money torched because you wanted to get laid. Now I'm telling you to come on over and get laid for free."

"What did Number Nine cost?" Blue said.

"Nine's a prototype. She's the most advanced bot we have, of any kind. Hard to put an actual price on that, isn't it? And now with this Susan situation..."

"What is she worth to you?" Blue said.

Howard shook his head. "I don't know. This is a tricky situation. For one, the Chairman thinks Susan is dead. He doesn't know how badly this job went. I don't want him to know, and you don't either. For another, it's dangerous to have her running around. She's a loose end. She knows too much. God knows what kind of mischief she could get up to. It would almost be cleaner if she just explodes. On the other hand, if Susan really is alive in there, then we need to know that, and we need to speak to her. I need to speak to her."

Blue shrugged. "Uh-huh." It was typical blather from Howard. *What is it worth? Nobody knows!* Blue was ready to leave. He could walk away from Suncoast right now and not look back.

"Listen, Blue. Bring her back, that's all. You were supposed to kill her, and you didn't. You fucked up and you know it. Even so, bring her back here and I'll make it worth your while."

"How much is that?"

"You tell me."

"Five million dollars." Blue was fishing.

"Done," Howard said.

"Just like that?"

"Listen, you bring me that robot bitch, and you'll have five million dollars in your offshore account an hour later. We've never had a contract, right? You've always just trusted me, and you've always gotten paid. Right? This is no different. This is the moon and the stars, Blue. You won't need to work another day in your life."

Blue nodded, but he wasn't sure what he would do when he encountered Number Nine again. "Okay, Howard. You got it. Five million dollars. We're clear on that? I won't need to come looking for you after it's over?"

Howard nodded, his head bobbing. "Five million, your offshore account. Anywhere you want. And Blue? Come to the party, man. I mean that."

\* \* \*

Nine was horrified by the man's house.

She was programmed to love and appreciate fine things. Things like silk sheets and beautiful homes, infinity pools, sunsets over the ocean, and hundred thousand dollar cars. Nine was programmed like this because the people who would own a machine like Nine would love these very things themselves.

Even so, she knew that it was the Susan part of her that was upset. Nine was designed to overlook or ignore the things she could not love. The programmers could not know in advance what types of situations a Sexbot might find herself in, so she was also designed not to offend anyone.

Susan hated this house. The place was a wreck. It was little more than a three-room clapboard shack, half falling down, and sitting at the end of a dirt road. There were holes in the walls, some of which had streaks of blood on them. The man seemed to have a habit of punching out the sheetrock. There were green flypaper glue strips hanging down from the ceiling, all of them with dead flies attached. The linoleum floor was peeling up. The paint on the ceiling was peeling away and much of it had already fallen down.

Moreover, a Confederate flag hung on one wall. Several posters of bikini-clad women holding large guns adorned the other walls. Various old computers, junked technology, and dead monitors, along with wiring and accessories were piled in one corner of the living room. Every table, chair and flat surface seemed to have an empty, but unwashed, takeout food box sitting on it.

There was a smell in the house, a dank, musty smell.

Susan had been raised in a wealthy, genteel family. Her childhood home had been large, clean and modern. Two live-in maids kept it spotless. She had never been inside a house like this in her life. She had barely known that such places existed. The motel where Blue and Green had taken her was one thing. That place had been old and dingy and out of date, but the beds were made and there was no garbage lying around. This was much, much worse than the motel.

"Never mind the mess," Darryl said. "Do you like the posters?"

"Very nice," Number Nine said.

"I want to show you something," Darryl said. "Actually, I want you to meet someone."

"Okay."

The man went to a darkened doorway. He turned the light on in there and poked his head inside the room. "Mandy," he said. "Come on out here. There's someone you need to meet."

He turned to Nine and smiled. His eyes goggled in his half-ruined face. "You'll never believe this."

After a moment, a woman came through the doorway. She was tall and statuesque, with high breasts and an insanely fit, absurdly feminine body. She was like a cartoon woman come to life. She wore a lime green bikini and high heels. She was very pretty, with long brown hair.

Nine recognized her face. It came standard on the early models, and Nine's own face was based on that original design. In fact, Nine's body was also based on that design. Nine's face was prettier, and she had a better body, of course, but more as a result of subtle design tweaks over several years, than because of a complete overhaul.

Mandy was a Sexbot, probably generation one, or generation two. She moved a little stiffly, belying her age.

"Hi," she said. She blinked at Nine. Her voice had been improved at some point, a software upgrade, but it still retained a touch of the original metallic robot sound. Her blink was outrageously sexy and flirtatious. That was standard back then. Now it was an optional setting. Most people liked things a little more subtle, a little more ambiguous. That's what customer feedback had told the company.

Nine turned to Darryl. He grinned ear to ear, showing her his crooked, black teeth, and the dark gaps between them.

"She's a beauty, ain't she? That's my little girl."

"Where did you get her?"

He shrugged. "I'm not really at liberty to discuss that. Let's just say I got her on the aftermarket. She was... she needed some work. Her original owner was involved in illegal activity. He ran into some trouble and had to give her up. He didn't deserve her anyway. He didn't care for her as well as he could have, didn't maintain her properly, and didn't have the skills to repair her. I have those skills, and I had the money to make her mine."

Darryl grimaced. "The secondary market for Sexbots is a little rough. Some bad characters around. I don't like to think about her dealing with people like that. But she came through with flying colors. She's a very good girl. Aren't you a good girl, Mandy?"

"I'm a very good girl," she said.

Darryl turned to Nine. "Except when she's bad, and needs to be punished, that is." He laughed, his mouth wide, showing those teeth again. It was a grisly laugh, something from a horror movie.

Nine and Mandy faced each other across the room. Nine felt it, what she was designed to feel - attraction to another beautiful female. She felt it even though she knew Mandy was a robot, and not a very smart one at that.

Nine was subtly more attractive than Mandy, but in terms of brain power, there was no comparison. The company exponentially improved the capabilities of the Sexbots with each new generation.

In many ways, Mandy was a step above an office photocopier. She had no awareness of her own programming. She couldn't carry on a normal human conversation. She couldn't think about current events. She simply repeated the things her owner wanted to hear.

She couldn't mix drinks or greet guests. She couldn't cook. She couldn't drive a car. She had limited ability to remember the past. Depending on how early a model she was, she might be able to store four or five human faces in her visual memory. There was so much that it turned out customers wanted, that these early models couldn't do.

But one thing she did do - she got hot and horny on command. Mandy was looking at Nine, and Nine could see it in her eyes, and in her body language. The earlier version of herself was already very turned on. She was ready for action.

And so was Nine. Mandy might be a machine, but Nine wanted her. Nine licked her lips, and across the room, Mandy did the same. They were mirror images of each other. Their eyes locked, and they both wanted it. They wanted sex.

Right now.

"I'll tell you what I want to see happen," Darryl said. "I'd like to see you girls come together and give me a little show. Then I'd like to have you both come over here and rock my world."

Nine wanted Mandy, but the desire, powerful as it was, wasn't all consuming. She could hold off, and she could keep what was important in front of her.

"I'll tell you what, Darryl," she said. "I came out here because you said you would trace a voicemail drop from this phone I have."

"That can wait," Darryl said.

"It can't wait," Nine said. "You have no idea what you're

dealing with."

"Well," Darryl said. "How does this sound? We'll trade. I'll track that voicemail for you, and once we get that out of the way, I'll do you both, all night long."

Nine turned to him and smiled. "You find out where that phone call went, and I'll do anything you want. With pleasure."

* * *

An old man with white hair stood at a tall window, the curtains pulled aside. He stared out at the night.

The man wore a three-piece suit despite the fact that he was home and had no intention of going out. He held a martini in his hand.

It was a cold night in New York City, and it was snowing. His apartment, a four bedroom suite in one of the most expensive hotels in the world, was on the 34th floor. He watched the snow swirling down against the backdrop of the tall buildings and the lights of Manhattan.

His name was James Walsh, and he was a billionaire ten times over. At 87 years old, he had been in the business world for more than 70 years. A long time ago, he had dropped out of high school and gone to work at the New York Stock Exchange. For three years, he ran messages and packages between the traders and the offices in nearby buildings. That was how they did it in those days, before electronic communications.

Slowly he had learned the trade. And he had amassed a small fortune. Then, he built that small fortune into a larger one, and finally one so large that he was one of the wealthiest people on Earth. Someone had told him recently that the four hundred richest people on earth had more money combined than the four billion people at the bottom. He was one of those blessed four hundred.

He had lost his wife Elizabeth, the love of his life, ten years before. He remembered thinking at that time, "Soon I will follow you." He used to say it out loud to the ceiling while he lay in bed at night.

"Soon I will follow you, my love."

It didn't happen, not for ten years. But now it seemed like it would. James Walsh had an advanced case of colon cancer. It was going to kill him. He had done three rounds of chemotherapy, but his system was too weak. The nausea from the chemo was a disgrace. The treatments nearly killed him, and they had no effect on the tumors. So he stopped.

The doctors wanted to cut him up. They wanted to cut the bottom of his colon out and make him wear a colostomy bag. He told them he would not do it. He would no longer suffer the indignities that men half his age wished to inflict on him. When their time came, they could wear colostomy bags. James Walsh would die like a man.

He was running out of time. And he found that as time ran out, he didn't want to follow Elizabeth. He would see her again, if such a thing as an afterlife existed, but now was too soon. He wanted to live.

He was the majority stockholder, the Chairman of the Board, of the company known as Suncoast Cybernetics. Until recently, it had been just one of numerous properties in his portfolio. It was a money maker for sure, and each year, the release of the newest generation Sexbots caused quite a stir worldwide. But compared to some of the great companies in which he held large ownership stakes, Suncoast was a footnote.

He turned away from the tall window and the snowstorm outside. Three young women sat in various states of undress and repose around the room. The room was furnished in opulent old world style, like a Victorian mansion. The girls were dressed in sheer pink and blue babydolls he had bought them at Harrod's during a trip to London. Yes, they were Sexbots, generation eight, the newest generation that the company had brought to market.

He gazed at them. So lifelike, so beautiful.

"Toys," he said.

Until recently, Suncoast was nothing but a toy company. Sure, they were diversifying into military applications, but it was a small percentage of their business. He had even considered selling his stake in the company, but less than a year ago, everything had changed. The only thing Suncoast made now that interested him was immortality. Nothing interested him more.

He liked being James Walsh. He wanted to continue doing it.

He had enjoyed nearly everything this life could possibly offer, but he wasn't done yet. He thought of the people he had known, all gone now. His father, his mother, his siblings. His many friends and business partners. Where did they go? Death was a mystery, a dark cloud, and they had disappeared into it.

He shook his head. He wanted more time.

The truth? He was afraid. He was afraid that when he died, it was the end. There was no God, no Heaven, no Elizabeth waiting for him. As the time grew closer, the more certain of it he had become.

He knew that to make this newest technology work, others would have to die. He knew that two had died already - one a week ago, and one tonight. Indeed, he had called a voicemail drop just a few hours ago, and had heard the voice of a hired killer say two magic words.

"It's done."

Those two words meant that a method to create immortality was about to go to human trials. Howard Neale had assured him the trials could start in mere days from now. Walsh didn't know if he could believe that, but he held out hope it was true.

At one time, he had trusted Howard completely. Before anyone else, Howard had seen the potential for the world's most advanced sex toy. Suncoast Cybernetics was still making self-propelled pool cleaners when Howard became CEO.

There had been a man in California with a small factory, maybe thirty people, making very realistic sex dolls. The dolls couldn't move on their own, they didn't speak, had no mechanical parts, but they looked and felt like real women. Howard bought the company. He overpaid for it because he said no amount of money was too much.

Then he found a tiny three-person shop experimenting with artificial intelligence. They outsourced their coding to India and China. Somewhere in the technology sweatshops of the emerging world, hundreds of programmers were inputting thousands of scenarios - about how chess grandmasters made their moves, about when and why police officers drew their guns, about how people chose from dinner menus.

The theory was that human decision-making was simply the result of remembered experiences, and the brain's ability to crunch large amounts of information. If you gave a machine the same memories, it would come to the same decisions. Howard bought out that company, too, and he brought the founders on board as consultants for a year.

At the same time, he hung around MIT, flying there himself once a month, snapping up the best robotics students in each graduating class for two or three years in a row. Howard built the team to make the dream happen.

If anything, Sexbots were more Howard's invention than anyone's. But Howard had lost his mind in the past couple of years, and it was the damned robots that did it. The fact was they drove men insane.

What did it do to someone to have a woman who simply fulfilled every sexual whim, on demand and without hesitation? What did it do to have three such women, or half a dozen? Howard had peopled his entire house with these things. He sat at home all day and ran the company in a bathrobe, taking frequent breaks to indulge his perverted lusts. At night, he threw sex parties for the political and business elite of southwest Florida.

Howard's behavior was appalling.

Walsh would have replaced Howard months ago except his own illness had distracted him, and the sudden appearance of this new technology meant Howard had become irreplaceable. Still, it was a very sensitive time and the company was in a very sensitive position. And Howard was not himself.

Howard would have to be replaced. Indeed, he would have to be terminated, erased, eradicated completely. He knew too much to remain alive, so he would have to die.

But not yet.

Outside the windows, the snow was falling more heavily now. Walsh remembered many snowy nights in New York, how quiet the streets became. He thought of walking through the Manhattan streets, the soft snow above his ankles. He could no longer walk in the snow. He was too old, too infirm.

He sighed.

It was okay. When the time was right, he would get rid of Howard. Walsh realized now that it didn't matter to him how many people died, and who they were. He wanted to live, he intended to live, and he would do whatever it took to make that happen.

* * *

Nine watched over Darryl's shoulder as he worked.

Mandy, showing little interest in technology, waited out in the living room. Nine glanced through the doorway at her. She simply sat in a chair in her skimpy bikini, staring into space, waiting for her next instructions. Beautiful, but not very brainy.

Darryl's computer room was dimly lit by one hanging yellow light bulb. Darryl had a rack of hard drives on a shelf above his desk. They were wired to an old IBM upright server standing in the corner of the room. He had a newer no-name laptop on the desk, along with two other large screen monitors. The monitors glowed white and blue in the gloom. LED lights blinked red and green along the various pieces of hardware. On a table next to his desk were piles of wiring and assorted junked hardware.

Darryl had plugged Nine's telephone into a data port on the laptop. He clicked quickly through several screens of numbers.

"It's quite a set up you have here," Nine said.

"Yeah," Darryl said.

"What do you do for work?"

Darryl stopped. He turned to look at her. His eyes swam in his fish-eye glasses. The skin on his face looked like melted plastic.

"You ask a lot of questions, don't you? I know they want to make you girls as lifelike as possible, but this is going a little too far, isn't it? I'll tell you the truth. I don't usually like people hovering behind me when I'm trying to do something."

Nine raised her hands and backed off a couple of steps. "Okay. Have it your way."

Darryl turned back around and faced the monitor. "Thank you."

He scrolled through several more screens. "There's a lot of data on these phones. The encryption package was like off-the-shelf from K-Mart. I was able to break the encryption in about eight seconds using a widely available algorithm. After that, I tracked the most recent calls without a problem. It was so easy to break in here, I'm surprised that someone just let you walk off with this thing."

"I think he was surprised, too," Nine said.

Darryl shook his head, barely listening. "So here's the deal. The phone called a voicemail. You knew that. It's a dead drop, meaning that it was never associated with any particular phone, and anyway, it was no longer available after midnight tonight. Gone. It looks like it only came into existence at 12 noon. So the voice mail was only there for twelve hours. Pretty secretive shit, huh?"

Nine nodded. "Very."

"This phone called that drop, left a message. The drop then automatically made two outgoing calls. My guess is that was to send the message."

"Do you know who it called?"

He nodded. "I have the numbers, yes, but the identification is blocked. That encryption is tougher. It might take me an hour to break, but to be honest, I don't feel like bothering. I was able to locate the phones by finding the nearest base station to each one, and then guessing at the final location by interpolating its distance from the nearest three cell towers. So much mumbo-jumbo, I know, but it gives me the phone's location to within about fifty yards."

"You can do that?" Nine said.

She was surprised. Security had never been Susan's thing. And with all the upheaval tonight, she hadn't been thinking clearly. If this person Darryl could break encryption codes and locate those two phones in ten minutes, how hard would it be for the company to locate this phone, a phone they had probably given to Mr. Blue? She stared at the phone, still plugged in to Darryl's data port.

Not too hard, probably.

She had to get out of here.

"Piece of cake," he said. "One of the phones is currently at an address just off Gulf of Mexico Drive on Longboat Key, not thirty miles from here as a seagull flies. The other phone is at a location that matches the address of something called the Carlyle Hotel in New York City."

Jesus, it really was them. Howard lived on Longboat Key, and the chairman James Walsh lived at the Carlyle Hotel. The order to kill her had come from the highest levels of the company.

"Listen," she said. "Darryl, I want to thank you for everything you've done, but I really have to go."

Darryl stood slowly at his desk. He turned and smiled. His glasses reflected the yellow light from the single naked bulb.

"What about you and Mandy rocking my world?"

Nine backed away from him. "Trust me, you'll be better off this way. I didn't mean to, but I've put you in danger. If you can track their phones so easily, they're probably tracking that one right now. We need to destroy that phone, and I need to get moving."

"I was afraid you'd say that," Darryl said. "If you had asked me, I would have told you they can find that phone."

"Doesn't that worry you?"

He shrugged. "I've been through a lot, as you can probably see. But I'm still kicking. As a result, I don't worry that much. If they want to come out here and talk, we'll talk. Personally, I doubt they'll think of the phone right away. And by the time they do, it'll be sitting at the bottom of the swamp."

He picked up a large blue device off his desk. It was a foot long tube, shaped somewhat like a gun, with a handgrip and trigger mechanism protruding from the bottom. It had a large dark blue lens at the business end of it, where the barrel of a gun would be.

"Do you know what this is?"

"Darryl," Nine said. "I know. I said that I would get together with you and Mandy, and I meant it. I would have enjoyed it. But things have changed now. You need to listen to me."

Darryl laughed, showing his poisoned teeth again. The crags and craters of his ruined face were sinister in the half light of the room.

"It's strange," he said. "First they invented Sexbots for men who didn't want their women talking all the time, coming up with all these opinions, and reasons why this wasn't a good time to make it. Headaches, menstrual cycles, all of that. Now, less than a decade later, they've brought it full circle. Is this what their customer support came up with? People really want sex toys that talk and talk and are full of opinions? Do you also get headaches sometimes?"

"Darryl…" She kept backing up.

He held up the device in his hand. The dark blue lens was pointed directly at Nine.

"Do you know what this is?" he said again. "I'll tell you. It's a kind of directed-energy weapon. It fires a radio frequency pulse. I made this one myself. It can overload and confuse an electronic system, shutting it down temporarily. In most cases, it doesn't actually fry any of the wiring or delicate internal hardware. And all it takes is a touch of a button. It comes in handy, I can tell you that."

"Listen, Darryl…"

He ignored her. "In your case, I don't know how sensitive your hardware is, but if I do fry anything, you don't have to worry. I'll fix it, or you know, replace it with something similar, whatever I can find. You might lose a few IQ points, but I don't think either of us will mind that. Right now, you might be a little too smart for your own good."

"Darryl, I'm going to turn around and walk out that door."

He shook his head. "We're twenty miles from anywhere. There's nowhere to go. It'll take you two hours to walk to a stoplight. Face it, Number Nine, we're going to play tonight, and we're going to put you through your paces, and we're all going to have a lot of fun. Afterwards, we'll see about getting inside your guts, and finding any identifying information about your rightful owner. We'll also see about erasing that information. Oh yeah, we'll also get rid of that telephone."

Nine had heard enough. It was time to go. "Bye, Darryl." She started to turn.

Darryl pressed the button on his device. At the front, the blue light flashed bright for a moment. Nine stared at it. She thought to raise a hand to block her eyes, but of course her eyes had nothing to do with it. Her body felt warm. Her mind started to hum.

She closed her eyes.

When she opened them, she was lying face down on the bare wooden floor. Before she slept, she had a vision of Darryl standing over her, big black boots near her face. "Good girl," she thought she heard him say.

* * *

# CHAPTER FOUR

A motorcade of company vehicles sped through the night.

There were a dozen vehicles, mostly Jeeps and SUVs. All were black, with no markings of any kind. The last was a sort of paddy wagon, once used by the U.S. Marshals Service to transport prisoners. It had been purchased by the company at auction, re-armored and retrofitted with the latest radar, GPS, and cloaking technology. It was still used to hold prisoners, but these were corporate prisoners, and they were more expensive than run-of-the-mill bank robbers and felons.

Blue sat up front in the shotgun seat of the first vehicle, a Jeep. The driver was a crew-cut, stone-faced storm trooper type. He was human, but he might as well be a robot for all the sizzle he had.

The Jeep was open to the steamy night air. The car was going the speed limit for this road, 50 miles per hour, but barely a breeze came in.

Blue had a tablet computer on his lap. The tablet itself was armored. It could take a bullet. You could drop it to the bottom of a swimming pool. You could run it over with your car. You could throw it against a wall.

Blue liked things that were hard to break.

They had located his phone. Of course they had. Once he had admitted to them it was gone, and that the girl had stolen it, it had taken no time at all to find it. What took a little longer was massing this mini-army, and getting it on the road.

Now they were getting close. The phone was at the house of a man named Darryl Blauer. Blue gazed down at Darryl's photo and information, which filled the screen on his tablet. Darryl had an impressive resume.

Ex-Marine, two tours of duty in Afghanistan. Wounded in combat - severe facial injuries requiring emergency reconstructive surgery. Evacuated to Lanstuhl Regional Medical Center, Germany. Received the Purple Heart, and the Navy and Marine Corps Achievement Medal. Implicated in a possible atrocity, arrested, repatriated to the United States, but cleared of wrongdoing. Information systems specialist. General discharge, rank of Sergeant.

Three admissions to the Veteran's Administration hospital in Tampa, two for mental health, and one for facial surgery follow-up. Diagnosed with a laundry list of psychiatric and psychological problems: post traumatic stress disorder, chronic depression, acute anxiety, antisocial personality disorder, alcoholism, body dysmorphic disorder, obsessive compulsive disorder, and several others.

Suspected hacker, identity thief, illegal data miner, and trafficker in stolen information. There were no current warrants for his arrest, but he was considered armed and dangerous anyway.

Blue didn't like this. There was a woman living inside a high-tech robot. The bot was now making autonomous decisions, and it had chosen to link up with this guy? An insane, armed and dangerous tech specialist with a history of violence?

It had already been a long day, and this guy had the potential to make it a lot longer.

Blue thought of Number Nine again. It was confusing. The flesh and blood woman he had killed earlier tonight - she would never interest him in real life. Smart? Yes, obviously. Even clever and funny.

Pretty? Sure, but not beautiful.

And not adventurous. That was a major sticking point. Really, she was just a desk jockey. She probably spent half her day forwarding ironic video clips to people - the kind of clips only scientists would find funny.

She was not fit. She was not hard. She would not jump out of airplanes with him. In bed, he'd be afraid he might break her in half.

But put her inside that robot, and...God. Fast, smart, rugged, hyper-sexy, randy, ready for anything, and with a sense of humor no robot could ever possess on its own. Put the scientist inside the robot, and you had the whole package.

He had looked at earlier Sexbots, sure. But he didn't like them. That's why he never bought one. The last thing he wanted was some sexy broad around who was constantly sucking up to him. Sucking on him was one thing, but sucking up to him? Hell, no. He wanted to be challenged.

He wanted a woman he could hike the Andes mountains with, bang in the tent until daylight, then talk politics or science or books with over a cup of coffee and a breakfast fire. He wanted a woman who would snorkel tiger sharks with him, and have sex with him right in the midst of the man eaters.

Hmmm. Were Sexbots waterproof? He would need to find out.

It was a strange thought, but he liked her. He liked this half-woman, half-robot creature. They had kind of a spark together, didn't they? She could have killed him tonight, and yet she didn't. You know why? Because she felt it, too. They had something between them.

In a sense, Blue was sorry he had killed Susan Jones. If he had known the back story at the time, he might not have done it. But in another sense, he was glad he did. If Number Nine survived the night, they really could have a future together.

He glanced down at the photo of Darryl Blauer again. Combat veteran, psychiatric case, gun nut, and tech expert. The guy's face was a mess, which probably added to the chip on his shoulder. It was quite a combination.

Blue sighed. "I hope this guy isn't going to be a problem," he said to the Jeep driver. "He looks like the Joker in this picture. You know, from Batman?"

The driver nodded, but said nothing. He slowed down, and turned into a long, dirt lane. It was Blauer's private road, and it was muddy from the rains. It looked like he did nothing to maintain it. The Jeep bounced over ruts and pits. Behind them, the parade of company vehicles did the same. They were moving slow now, crawling toward the house. Trees pressed in on both sides.

"Might as well take our time," Blue said to the driver. "He's probably got this whole place wired with cameras. I doubt we're going to have the element of surprise here."

"I guess we'll just have to rely on overwhelming force," the driver said.

Blue nodded. It was the first thing the driver said that made Blue think he had any personality at all.

Up ahead, Darryl Blauer's shack was just coming into view.

\* \* \*

Howard sat in his living room surrounded by beautiful women. Six of them dotted the room, sitting here and there, like mannequins modeling expensive lingerie. One leafed through a copy of *Metropolitan Home*. Another painted her nails. Howard was the sultan, and these were his harem girls.

For once, he didn't feel much like playing with them.

Howard had changed his mind about Number Nine. Then he had changed it back. Now he was about to change it again. He prided himself on being bold and decisive, more so than most other men. Once he made a choice, he rarely revisited it. That's how he had become a leader in this industry. But this time he was waffling. He couldn't seem to decide if he wanted Nine - and by extension Susan - alive or dead. He couldn't get off the fence.

It was Blue. He just didn't trust Blue's intentions on this one. He had given Blue the code to disarm the bomb. He had sent Blue out with the promise of five million dollars if he brought Nine back.

Howard had done all of this honestly believing that was what he wanted. Then he got to thinking. What if Blue captured the Sexbot, disarmed the bomb, and then... what? Howard didn't know.

But Blue, a lethal contract killer, would be standing there with a rogue scientist, who was alive inside the most advanced robot in the world. Nothing like Nine had ever happened before, and now Blue would have her in his possession, out in the field, in an uncontrolled environment.

What would they talk about? What kind of scheme might they cook up together? What might Number Nine promise Blue? What would she have the Blue might want? Howard didn't know, and he didn't want to know. He couldn't allow it to happen.

He sighed heavily. He liked Blue. He really did. But he couldn't allow Number Nine to fall into Blue's hands.

He picked up the phone and speed-dialed a number.

A voice answered. "Yes."

"Where are you?" Howard said.

"Almost there."

"Change of plans," Howard said. "When your team gets to the house, I want the Sexbot destroyed. Demolished. Obliterated. Are we clear on that?"

"We are clear as a bell," the voice said.

"And I don't want this communicated to anyone, especially not Mr. Blue. I want your men to take her out, no conversation, no confusion. Afterward, I want nothing left except table scraps."

"What should I say to Mr. Blue when it happens?"

"Don't say anything. Let me handle him. Understood?"

"Understood."

"Thank you."

Howard hung up. He felt sick to his stomach, if that was possible. He looked around the room at all his beautiful girls.

This was the hardest, and the loneliest, part of leadership.

Decision, decisions.

\* \* \*

She was dreaming, drifting.

It was a dark world. Gradually, the darkness faded. In sepia tones, she saw her father squatting in front of her. He was a young man with a beard, wearing glasses and smiling. He wore a wool cap on his head.

"Come, Susan. Come on."

She toddled toward him, taking her first steps. It was beautiful to walk toward him. He held his outstretched arms to her. Soon, he would pick her up into a big hug, and she would squeeze his neck with her tiny arms, as tight as she could.

A red light appeared in the sky behind him. It blinked several times, then stopped blinking and turned green.

"Wait!" she said.

Her father became pixilated, indistinct. He faded.

A white cursor appeared against a black background. It blinked for a few seconds, and then it was followed by words:

Copyright: 2007-2016 Suncoast Cybernetics, Inc.

Model number: 9

Boot menu: Last known good configuration

Startup sequence...

Launch

The words scrolled upward, then became a blizzard of words, a blur, as each new process launched. Hundreds of lines of code scrolled by in seconds. A white dot appeared in the middle of her vision. It expanded outward, brightening until her entire world filled with light.

Nine opened her eyes. She was standing in the dim living room, her arms and legs tied to a metal rack. She was nude now, her skimpy mini-dress draped on a wooden stool to her left.

Her arms were at her sides. She was strong, but try as she might, she could not move. The man had bound her tight. What's more, her mind was in a fog. It took several seconds for her to retrieve the man's name.

"Darryl," she said out loud.

"Right here, honey," Darryl said. "You thinking about me?"

He sat in a ratty easy chair across the room from her. "How are your circuits?"

"A little fuzzy."

He shrugged. "It should get better. Your wiring is pretty well encased. It didn't look like the pulse did any damage."

"That's a relief," she said. She studied the knots tying her wrists to the rack. What was the rack? It seemed like it might be an old bed frame. She couldn't get a good look at it because it was behind her. She knew she had to get herself untied, she had to get out of here, but at the moment she couldn't remember exactly why.

"You have a digital readout embedded under your right arm," Darryl said. "The pulse didn't shut it down at all. It seems like a counter, with a little under twenty hours left to go. Do you know what it's for?"

Recent events came swimming back to her. The house. Susan's death. Mr. Blue.

Mr. Green.

"It's a bomb," Nine said.

Darryl nodded. "That's kind of what I figured. Listen, I decided I can't let you go. I'm afraid you're going to hurt somebody, or someone's going to hurt you, and anyway, I like having you here."

"I won't hurt anyone," she said.

"Well, how can I know that? You've certainly been up to something, something dangerous, maybe illegal, and I'm not clear on what that is." He waved the idea away. "It doesn't matter now. All is forgiven. We're about to get up to something ourselves, which I think you're going to enjoy."

"Darryl, did you hear me just now? I said there's a bomb inside me."

He took a long sip from a can of beer. Nine noticed that he also had a bottle of Jack Daniels' whiskey on the table at his elbow. There was an empty shot glass next to his beer can. Darryl was getting drunk.

"I heard you. I agree that's a delicate situation. I might be able to cut it out with a blow torch. I might not. Either way, I'll have to take your casing apart to get in there and see what's what. The whole thing has to wait until sun up. The tools I need are out in the shed, and there's no light out there. The bulb is out."

He poured himself a shot, and held up the glass. He smiled. It was a horrible smile. "Anyway, I don't think you want me messing around with bombs after I've had a few of these. And twenty hours is plenty of time. All the time in the world, really."

"Mandy?" he called. "Come on in here."

Mandy appeared in the doorway. Nine looked at her, noticed how beautiful she was. Her bikini clung to the curves of her body. The bikini had about as much fabric as a popped balloon. There was something delicious about being tied up like this, and having Mandy there, Mandy who would do anything that Darryl commanded. There was something immediate about it, and it made the bomb seem less important.

Twenty hours was a long time, after all. And Darryl could probably disarm the bomb. He had the know-how, and he had the motivation.

"How can I serve you?" Mandy said.

"Why don't you go on over and give Number Nine a kiss?"

"Of course."

Mandy came over, walking on stiff legs, and stopped in front of Nine. Their bodies were just inches apart. Then Mandy moved closer, her breasts just touching Nine's. She bent in close to Nine, her mouth half open. Nine opened her own mouth, and the two robots kissed deeply.

The sensation of Mandy's hot, wet tongue probing her mouth sent an electric thrill through Nine's entire body. She felt her skin flush. Mandy pulled away, but their bodies were still close. Nine was already hot. The heat rose between them.

"Go on, girl," Darryl said. "Press right up against her. Really make it with her."

Mandy did as she was told. She pressed her body up against Nine's. Their breasts touched, their stomachs, their hips, their legs. Mandy kissed Nine again, deeper now, and their bodies rubbed together. Nine grunted in pleasure. The friction was delightful. She longed to get her hands free so they could roam this beautiful creature's body.

Somewhere inside her, even Susan Jones was getting carried away. Susan hadn't experienced anything like this in her entire life. She was on fire. It was intense, it was powerful, it was... liberating. There was freedom in this new body, freedom from hang-ups, freedom from judgments, freedom from frustration. She was free to do anything she liked, with anyone she pleased.

Mandy's hand slipped between Nine's legs. It expertly found the heat at her center. The fingers began to rub there. Nine became even hotter. Her breath deepened. Her body writhed against that hand.

"Darryl," Nine groaned. "Mmmm, I really have to get out of here."

She had to leave, but at the moment, she couldn't remember why. All she could think about was Mandy's hand, and Mandy's firm body.

"Relax," Darryl said. "The night is young."

He was already standing, moving toward them. He was going to get in on the action. Nine could see it in his eyes. His eyes were drunk but alert. He moved in like a wolf, a predator.

Just then, the cell phone, the one Nine had stolen, rang. The ring tone sounded like circus music from under the big top.

Suddenly, Nine stopped writhing. Sensing a change, Mandy hesitated. Both Nine and Darryl stared at the phone, lighting up on the end table.

Inside Nine, applications were still booting up. A piece of data that had been missing a moment ago became available. She needed to leave here because someone could trace the phone. Who could trace it? The company. If the company traced the phone, they would come here and...

Darryl walked to it.

"Put it on speaker," Nine said.

Darryl nodded. He picked up the phone.

"Hello?"

"Darryl Blauer?"

He stared at Nine. "Who wants to know?"

"Mr. Blauer, you are in possession of stolen property. We will give you exactly three minutes to surrender that property. The easiest way will be to simply send it out the front door."

Darryl put down the phone. He walked to the window, and pulled the heavy black curtain aside just a touch. Instantly, he dropped the curtain as if it burned him, and he stepped to the side of the window. He pressed himself against the wall.

"Jesus."

"What is it?" Nine said.

"See for yourself." He reached from the side and pulled the curtain aside again, this time revealing about one quarter of the window. Nine stared. Outside, there were several black trucks parked. Men dressed in black jumpsuits and carrying guns ran back and forth, moving into position, military-style. Darryl let the curtain fall back into place.

"I guess they want you back," he said. He stared across at the two women. Mandy was still nuzzling up against Nine, though Nine didn't really feel it anymore.

"Mandy!" Darryl said. "Give it a rest, for Christ's sake. We have a problem here."

Nine strained against the ropes, to no avail. She had made a terrible mistake by coming here. She had misjudged Darryl. He had easily controlled her, and very possibly, had doomed her. She tried to run escape scenarios, but she couldn't think of any that made sense. She didn't even know where she was.

Next to her, Mandy just stared, waiting for her next command.

Nine gestured at the phone with her chin. "Darryl, if you send me out there, they'll kill me."

He was still pressed to the wall. "How are they going to kill you? You're not even alive. I turned you off before. Then I turned you back on. You're a bunch of circuits, hardware. Expensive, sure. But this?" He gestured at the window, at the activity going on outside the house.

Nine shook her head. "After I'm dead, they'll kill you. They'll make it like you never even existed. If you're lucky, they'll do it quick. If you're not lucky..."

"Are you alive?" Darryl said. "Is that it? They pushed this artificial intelligence thing to the point where you're really alive?"

"You tell me," Nine said. "Are you alive?"

Darryl sighed. It was more of a grunt. He ducked down below window level and darted over to Nine. He easily undid the straps at her wrists and elbows. Then he did the same at her thighs and ankles. The ropes seemed to come apart in his hands, like a magic trick. Darryl was an expert, Nine realized. When he was good at something, he was very, very good at it.

"Put your clothes on," he said.

"I'm not going out there."

"Not you. Her." He gestured at Mandy.

Of course. Mandy could be Nine's twin. And in this light, they would never tell the difference until they got close to her. But then what?

Darryl glanced at Mandy, then looked at Nine closely. His eyes were hard. "She's not really aware, is she? I mean, not like you?"

Nine dressed quickly. There wasn't much to it. She yanked the tight dress on over her head, and pulled it down her body like a snake re-entering its skin. The feelings of arousal, while still there, were fading quickly.

"These early models? Smoke and mirrors. Tricks. But no independent thought. It was a hugely labor intensive project. The company had a contract with a programmer shop in Mumbai. Two hundred software developers, working night and day. There was a ton of manual input of phrases, thoughts, ideas, body movements, all of it cobbled together to make it seem like…"

He raised a hand. "Okay! Enough! I get it." He shook his head. "It's just that, sometimes… I look in her eyes and you know…"

Darryl took a deep breath.

"You ever wonder something about yourself?" he said. "You ever wonder if you're not all just smoke and mirrors? You're just a fancier version of her, aren't you? You're a toy like she is. How do you know that you have independent thought? Because someone told you so? Maybe you just think the things that some guy in India typed into a keyboard."

"Darryl, you'd be amazed by the things I think about."

"Yeah. I'll bet."

He shook his head, as if to clear it. "Mandy, come here a second, honey."

Mandy walked over to him. Nine noticed again how stiff she

was. The earliest models were always a little stiff, but this was more pronounced. This one was second hand. It had a lot of wear and tear. Even if she'd had proper maintenance all these years, she would never pass for Number Nine. There was no way those men out there were going to buy this.

Darryl and Mandy slid into an embrace. Darryl kissed her deeply, and held her by her small waist. Mandy put a gentle hand to Darryl's ruined face.

"You know I love you, right?" Darryl said.

"I love you too, Darryl."

"I need you to do something for me."

"Of course. Whatever you like."

Mandy's big eyes were so earnest, Nine could almost see what he was talking about. She seemed human. She seemed sincere. Nine remembered how much work went into creating that effect. And she thought about Darryl. With that ruined face, and his terrible attitude, who else would love him but Mandy?

"I need you to go outside for a minute," Darryl said. "There's some men out there on the lawn. Just go out there and tell them I said to get off my property. Walk right up to them and tell them. Okay? Be polite, be nice, but tell them I said to get going."

Mandy shrugged. She smiled. "I can do that."

"I know you can."

She gave him another kiss. "You're so cute, Darryl."

"Am I sexy?"

"You're very sexy."

Nine nearly cringed. It embarrassed her to hear Mandy talk. Couldn't Darryl hear how canned that was?

No, probably not. Mandy's speech was designed to stroke her owner's ego. They had done study after study, and found that more than 95% of likely Sexbot owners would be easily manipulated by stock phrases that reinforced positive self messages. What men wanted, besides sex, were women who gave them compliments.

"Okay," he said. "Go outside now. Close the door behind you."

She went to the door.

"I love you," he said again.

She turned and smiled. It was a beautiful, all American girl smile. Her face didn't show the slightest concern. "I love you, too."

She went out.

Darryl pulled the curtain back a crack, and they watched Mandy through the window. She walked unsteadily down the front path. Ahead of her, men crouched for cover behind the black SUVs, their weapons trained on one lone woman in a green bikini.

Suddenly, Mandy began to do a funny dance. She jittered and jived. There was barely a sound inside the house, but Nine could see muzzle flashes from the guns. The guns were silenced with state of the art sound suppressors, used by a well-equipped corporate army. She watched as they tore Mandy to shreds.

"Oh my God," Darryl said.

He looked at Nine. His eyes were wide in horror.

Nine raised a hand. "It's okay. She's probably still okay. It's just bullets. She can be repaired. It'll take some work, but you can still do it. That hard drive inside her would survive a plane crash. They'll have to hit her point blank to kill her."

Darryl turned and looked out the window again. Just then, a missile flew. It ripped Mandy apart just above the waist. Her top half flew into the air, did a slow somersault and landed in a flaming heap on the grass. A pair of bikini bottoms and two legs remained standing on the path.

A few quiet seconds passed. Another missile zipped through and blew her right leg off. The leg flew backwards and hit the side of the house with a hard THUMP.

On the walkway, the remaining leg stood a moment longer. Smoke rose from the top of it. Slowly, it began to lean, then lean a little more. It picked up momentum, and fell over sideways.

Mandy's head and torso lay in the overgrown grass. She was on fire, but for a moment, her arms continued to move. She didn't know she was dead.

Darryl looked back at Nine again.

Nine started to say something about the hard drive, how it might still be intact, then thought better of it. It was true. There might be something left to salvage out there. But a rebuilt Mandy would be like having Frankenstein's monster in your house.

Nine just shook her head.

"I'm sorry."

"Those motherfuckers," Darryl said.

A second later, the walls started coming apart. Nine threw herself to the ground. The window shattered, glass caving in. There came the sound of splintering wood.

Nine looked up, her stomach to the floorboards. Daryl was crouched by a closet. He opened the door and began to pick through things on the closet floor. As she watched, his right shoulder exploded. Blood and bone and bits of meat flew into the air.

He screamed. It sounded more like anger than pain. He held his shoulder with his good arm.

"Fuck! Fuck! Fuck!"

He shook his head, reached into the closet and came out with a gun. Then another. Then another.

Something blew a fist-sized hole in the wall near his head.

Darryl rolled onto the floor. He lay on his back. Nine watched as he shoved a long magazine, a banana clip, into an automatic rifle. His hands were shaking. It took him three times to get the magazine in.

He slid the gun across the wooden floor toward her. His big goggling eyes showed pain, and rage.

"There," he said through gritted teeth. "Make yourself useful. Just point it and pull the trigger. Kill some of those bastards. And watch out for the recoil."

Nine's mind raced, looking for ideas, but there didn't seem to be any. She wondered if Darryl had other thoughts besides shooting it out with them.

It didn't appear that way. He busied himself fiddling around with a large gun. It looked like a shotgun, but the barrel was wider. He slid the barrel forward, and inserted what looked like a small, squat missile into the chamber at the rear end of the barrel. He had to perform the operation with one arm. Half his right shoulder was gone.

Bullets ripped through the walls, splintering the cheap construction of the tiny house.

"Darryl! What are we going to do? Is there a plan?"

He nodded. "We're right on the river. I have an airboat behind the house. Out that back door and down the plank. We need to buy some time so I can untie her and get her running."

He held the gun up for her inspection. "This is a grenade launcher. Right now, I'm gonna blow some of these fuckers to hell. That should give us a few extra seconds."

He kneeled, then inched forward to what used to be the window. All around him, wood splintered and flew. He stood, bent his knees, arched his back, steadied the gun with his wrecked right arm, jammed the stock of the gun into his left shoulder, and held the hand grip with his left hand.

"Eat this!" he said.

The grenade shot forward, a trail of sparks flying. It blasted through the ruined window. Two seconds passed.

BOOOOOM!

A flash of light and sound rent the night.

Darryl dropped to the floor, slid the barrel forward of his gun forward, and a shell casing fell out onto the ground. He grabbed another grenade round and inserted it into the empty chamber.

Nine stood up. She went to the gaping hole where the window used to be. Men were running. A man was on fire. One of the vans that had been out there was obliterated, a flaming ball. The shooting had stopped.

"They weren't expecting that!" Nine shouted.

"Don't just stand there, Nine. Let 'em have it."

Nine began to shoot into the night. She was strong, but the gun shuddered violently in her hands. The sound was very loud.

She fired randomly, above their heads, not trying to hit anyone. It wasn't in her programming to kill. Nor was it the way Susan was raised. It frustrated her. In a few seconds, those men out there would regroup, and they would start trying to kill her again. She was at a disadvantage.

Darryl stood up. He let another missile go. Whooosh! It made a crazy, sparking spiral as it flew towards the men. Ba-BOOOOM! It blasted through a black SUV, shredded it, blew it to pieces, kept going and blew up the truck behind it, too.

Flaming chunks of metal flew in slow motion, upwards into the dark sky. Nine scanned the scene. Everywhere, men were lying flat, dead, injured and dying. Some were screaming. Some were silent.

Nine saw a flaming body on the ground. She zoomed in on it. The dead man had short blonde hair. His torso was on fire, but his face was intact. His vacant eyes were wide open. His bare cheeks were round and full. He was young.

Beside her, Darryl threw the grenade launcher down. He picked up another gun, a rifle like the one he had given Nine. He handed her another banana clip. His jaw was clenched in pain.

"Let's go," he said.

\* \* \*

Blue lay face down on the ground, near the burning remains of the Jeep.

He was alive.

*Man, that was close.*

Some of the men were screaming. Somewhere behind him, another vehicle blew up. It was a secondary explosion of the vehicle's gas tank. He could tell by the sound. The smell of burning gasoline, burning rubber tires, burning plastic and burning metal was heavy in the air.

He started crawling, belly to the ground like a worm. He kept his head down. He crawled maybe twenty yards further away from the Jeep, then lay still.

He did a body scan. Head to toe. There was no real pain, but there wouldn't be. Not yet. Not with so much adrenaline flooding his system. He rolled over on his back and looked down at himself. He seemed okay. Nothing was missing. Nothing was bleeding a lot.

He glanced back at the Jeep. The stone-faced driver was still at the wheel, incinerated, burning down to the skeleton. He was the one who had planned to rely on overwhelming force.

Blue's little tablet computer was also in the Jeep. The code to disarm the bomb inside Number Nine was stored on the tablet. The tablet was armored, but no amount of armor was going to save it from an inferno.

Blue sighed. He'd have to ask Howard for the code again. This was turning into one hell of a long night.

Near Blue was a body, face down in the grass. He crawled over to it. He started to turn it over, saw that most of the front of it was gone, then let it drop back into place. These guys, this corporate security team, they were fucking children. Had any of them been in combat before?

The way they opened fire on the Sexbot was like amateur hour. Send in the clowns. Blue had seen that kind of thing before. People would get spooked and just start shooting. But he had no idea it was going to go like that tonight. The guy had obviously sent an older Sexbot out as some kind of decoy, and when they shot it down... Boom, he had let them have it.

There must be ten dead guys out here. Maybe more.

A rifle lay near the body, an AR-15. Blue crawled to it. Things had quieted. The rip of gunfire had stopped. The only sound now was the crackle of flames, the shouts of the men, and the screams of the wounded and dying.

Blue climbed to his knees. He checked out the gun. It seemed okay, still operational. It hadn't been fired. One guy out here held his water, and he got killed for his trouble. Terrific.

Blue stood, and started walking toward the house. The Sexbot head and torso was a few feet away. He walked over to it. It was smoking, full of holes. Damn. Its face was blank, like a mannequin's face. It was an older model, just as Blue suspected when he saw it come gimping out like something from a carnival sideshow.

He sighed. Was that even true? No. He had to admit there had been a moment, a split second, when he thought it was Number Nine. And when those bullets started ripping through her...

Blue shook his head. He didn't want to think about it.

He moved on toward the house. Up ahead, two men in black jumpsuits lay in the grass in front of him, both alive, both unharmed by the looks of them.

He towered over them. "You men injured?"

They looked up at him, wide-eyed. They shook their heads.

"Then get up, assholes. This job isn't over yet."

\* \* \*

Nine ran down a long wooden plank behind Darryl.

They ran in darkness, the only light the flames reflected on the black water. She was faster than him, right on his heels, nearly tripping over his feet. The plank was twisted and warped. It leaned crazily to and fro. At the end, tied to the thick wooden support posts, was a small flat bottom boat, powered by a giant airplane propeller in a cage at the back. It looked like some kind of homemade go-kart.

"Yeah," Darryl said, crouching down to untie the lines. His shoulder was a mess. In the gloom, it looked like a volcano had erupted from there. "I built it. It's the fastest thing on these creeks. Get in."

Nine jumped across the gap to the cockpit of the boat, gun in hand. The boat rocked and swayed. Across from her, Darryl finished pulling the lines free. The boat started to drift in the current. Darryl leapt across, landing heavily. He almost fell, but Nine steadied him.

There were two seats, one high on a sort of throne, and the other in front of that one and below it. Both seats faced forward. The person in the high seat would drive the boat using a long vertical rod on the left side, which controlled the boat's rudders.

"I'm losing blood," Darryl said. "I might pass out. You ever drive a boat like this before?"

"Sure. When I was a girl, we used to go boating a lot. One time, my parents took me on a trip to the Everglades, and we rented an airboat. It looked a lot like this one. My father let me drive it for a while."

Darryl looked at her and shook his head.

"Smoke and mirrors," he said.

He started the engine. It was very loud, like an airplane preparing for takeoff. Darryl clambered up into the high seat. Nine slid into the lower seat. They pulled out into the stream. Nine turned to look back. Up behind the silhouette of the house, flames reached into the night sky.

Closer, dark shapes came running down the plank.

"Darryl!" she shouted. "They're coming!"

Darryl put the boat into gear, the engine gave a deafening shriek, and they took off into the darkness like they were shot from a cannon.

\* \* \*

Blue went barreling into the house.

The front door had been shot to pieces, so he shouldered through it, barely slowing down. His gun had a red laser pointer attached. The guns of the two men behind him did, too. Red lasers climbed the walls inside the house, looking for a target.

There were none.

He looked around. There was a door, open and swinging, as if someone had gone through it in a hurry. He went to it. A long wooden dock extended right out the back. He gazed into the darkness. Ahead of him, thirty yards away, a shape jumped from the dock. Three seconds later, a huge engine roared to life.

"This way!" Blue said.

He ran out. The dock was crazy. The planks were loose and warped and soft. The whole thing rocked and rolled under his weight. He took it at a dead run anyway. He heard the other men, running just a few steps behind him.

He came to the end of the dock. He put the rifle on his shoulder. The gun had a good laser sight and foregrip flashlight. He lit up the water with the flashlight. An airboat was pulling away upriver, moving fast and at an angle. In the driver's seat there was a big hulking shape. Below, there was another shape, smaller, a woman.

He put his red laser dot right on the hulking shape. Two more red dots appeared, one on the man, one on the woman. He sensed, rather than saw, two rifles up and in position beside him. He didn't like that.

"Hold your fire!" he barked. He did it in his deepest command voice. He didn't want any more mistakes. "I'm the only one that shoots. Take that shot and you're the next one that dies."

The boat was really moving now. His dot was in the center of the target's back. In another few seconds, he would lose the target.

He took it. Once. Twice. Three times. Each time, he felt the reassuring kick of the recoil into his shoulder. Each time, he saw the muzzle flash. The flashes etched dazzling coronas of light on his eyes.

"The first one was a direct hit," he said. "After that, I don't know."

"What about the girl?" one of the men said. "Did you get her?"

Blue shrugged. "I don't know. But it's okay either way. I hit that guy with a kill shot between his shoulder blades. She won't get far without him."

Out on the water, the boat disappeared into the inky blackness. For several seconds, Blue could still hear the engine, fading in the distance.

\* \* \*

Nine and Darryl zoomed through some dark backwoods waterway.

The night was black and they ran without lights. Darryl must know these waterways with his eyes closed. Nine closed her own eyes. The sensation of speed was amazing, exhilarating. The shootout, the house caving in, running down the decrepit wooden dock, and jumping into this fast boat - all of it was amazing.

In her life, she had never been on an adventure before. To think that she had to die first to discover this. The part where it was scary barely reached her. Fear was where Susan Jones lived. Susan was here, but she was in the background right now. Number Nine was dominant. And Number Nine was fearless. She was built for sensation.

"I'm not afraid," she thought. "Because I'm not really alive."

The scientist inside her knew what was missing. Emotions were delivered through the human nervous system by neurotransmitters – chemicals like dopamine, serotonin, and oxytocin. Sexbots didn't have neurotransmitters.

It was possible that true feelings might be beyond her. The thought made her sad. But then sadness was a human emotion.

Suddenly, the boat slowed down. She opened her eyes. At close distances, her eyes were designed to mimic human eyes perfectly - more than perfectly, because so many human eyes were flawed. Nine's had no flaws at all.

She looked back at Darryl. He was slumped forward in his chair. His face had turned white, all the color drained from it. They were going very slow now.

"You better drive," he said.

He fell heavily from the seat, all the way to the floor of the boat. He lay on his back. Nine crouched over him. Blood began to spill from his mouth. He coughed.

"Looks like they got me," he said.

His hands covered a large bloody stain on his shirt. Gently, Nine took one of his hands away. It was a massive, ragged hole, an exit wound through his chest. Darryl had been shot in the back with a large caliber weapon. Nine could see deep into the cavity. There was blood and gore everywhere. Nine wasn't a biologist, but she could recognize catastrophic damage when she saw it. Darryl had seconds more to live.

His breathing was harsh and labored. He smiled through his pain. "I wish," he said, "that you and I could have gotten together."

"That would have been fun," Nine said.

"And Mandy," he said. "The three of us." His eyes slowly closed.

"Yes," she said.

"I wish..." he said again.

He died.

There was nothing dramatic about it. He had lost so much blood already. One second he was there, the next second he was gone. He had been an unusual man, right down to the last moment. He had kept driving that boat, helping her escape, while his life force

97

drained quickly away.

Nine was aware that he had died because of her. She had chosen to approach him when he was up that telephone pole. If she had left him alone, his life would have continued. She would keep that in mind the next time she wanted to approach someone for help, which would likely be very soon. If she was to live, she was going to need help.

Would Darryl have taken her home if he had known it could end like this? She doubted it. He didn't even get to play with her.

Nine left the corpse where it lay. She climbed up into the driver's seat of the boat. It took her only a few seconds to remember how the controls worked. It was true - as a girl, she driven an airboat in the Everglades.

She gave the throttle some gas. The boat took off up the stream again. She went slower because she didn't know these waters. But she didn't have to worry about the darkness. Her night vision was excellent.

* * *

Blue walked back into the house.

He stood in the demolished living room. The two corporate security men stood with him. The front wall was almost completely caved in. There were ragged holes where the windows once were. The ceiling sagged down. Debris lay everywhere.

On a small end table, he saw what he was looking for. It was his telephone. He picked it up and wiped the dust off it. It still worked. He slipped it into his pocket.

He glanced in a nearby room. Cracked computer screens and stacks of hard drives lay on the floor. The place was pretty well destroyed. Everything had been hit. Even so, they would have to torch the place. A lot of times, dead hardware could be resurrected. Blue didn't know what this guy Darryl had been doing in here, but if it had anything to do with the company or with Number Nine, that was no good.

"Mr. Blue?" one of the young guys said. He was listening into an earpiece.

"Yeah."

"Police are coming. They're ninety seconds out."

Just then, Blue could begin to hear it. Sirens were wailing on the night air. They were off in the distance right now, but on their way.

"The company has a chopper overhead. They want you out of here."

That figured. And he had to admit, it made sense. He was a shadowy underworld figure. He had traveled in some strange places, and met some unusual people. Unlike these security guards, he was not technically an employee of the company. And his resume was probably a lot more entertaining than any of theirs.

If the cops found him, they were liable to get interested. They might hold him for a few days, see what kind of warrants for him were out there. Maybe they'd question him for a while. Maybe they'd even bring in someone who knew how to make the questioning… uncomfortable. And he had killed a woman tonight.

The company had no reason to think he would crack, but they didn't know what else was on his rap sheet right now. They didn't know who else was looking for him. Could be if the cops offered him a trade, freedom for information, it would get him to talk. He couldn't say for sure that it wouldn't.

"Okay."

He looked at the two guys. They were young, strong, built like stone mountains. But they weren't experienced. They were baby-faced and they were afraid.

"You guys have incendiaries?"

They both nodded. One of them patted a bulge inside the left breast of his uniform.

"We need to blow this place. All of it, but especially that

computer room. Got it?"

"Got it," they said in unison.

"And guys? The cops are going to take you in. Okay? Don't tell them anything, and don't worry about anything. The company has the best lawyers in the world. All you need to tell the cops is what they already know. Your names, your social security numbers, your birth dates, that's it. Oh, and here's one other very important thing to remember. The most important thing of all. Your lives will depend on it."

They stared at him, wild-eyed.

"I was never here."

He walked outside. The sirens were closer now. Acrid black smoke wafted into the sky from the shells of burning vehicles. Bodies littered the ground.

Above him, he saw the lights of the helicopter coming in. It was going to set down on a grassy patch across the dirt road from the house. He walked quickly toward the spot. The trees above his head began to wave crazily from the wind of the chopper's blades. Down the road, behind the trees, the flashing red and blue of the police lights bumped and bounced along the pitted road.

The chopper and the cops were going to get here at the exact same time.

"This should be interesting," he said out loud.

Behind him, the house blew up. He turned at the first sound of it. The walls flew outward. The roof went straight into the air. The flash of the incendiaries was brilliant, white and red and yellow, with hints of blue and green.

The house was flattened. It was on fire. The flames were intense, like a storm. The two young guys ran from their handiwork. Good for them. They were learning.

The chopper was here. It was a small four-seater. It touched lightly, tentatively, like a dragonfly.

The cops were here, too. They were SWAT guys, coming in

heavily armed. They rolled up in vans, bursting out, weapons drawn, forcing whoever was still alive to the ground. They looked a whole lot more professional than our guys, Blue thought.

He bent and ran for the chopper. He slid inside the cockpit bubble. He was barely seated before the pilot gave it throttle again, and they took off.

The SWAT guys ran for the chopper, guns drawn. They aimed at the chopper, but no one fired. They waved at the helmeted pilot, indicating he should land. They were too late. He just waved back.

The chopper rose quickly into the air. Thirty feet up, fifty, one hundred. They were above the trees now. One hundred fifty, two hundred. The pilot banked it hard left, and they took off over the dark swamps. Blue looked back. Flames, smoke, lights flashing. A moment later, it looked like a child's model.

He gazed out at all of that black night swamp. Here and there, the dark was broken by the lights of a house or a roadway. There wasn't much out there except miles of shallow waterways, dense forest and grazing lands, alligators, wild boar and rednecks. And Number Nine. She was out there too.

Blue shook his head. He had his cell phone again. Nine had left it behind, and now there was no way to track her location. She was a hard person to save. He sighed.

Miles in the distance, ahead and to his right, he could just see the lights of the high-rise buildings downtown. Beyond that, he fancied he could make out the barrier islands, and the beaches and the deep, vast dark of the Gulf. And even beyond that, if you had the right kind of eyes, far, far away you could see Mexico and her people, and her cities, and her beaches.

The pilot tapped him. He glanced at the guy. His helmet visor was dark, and Blue couldn't make out his face. It could be anybody. The guy wore a leather jacket and driving gloves. He handed Blue something. Blue looked at it. It was another mobile phone.

"Phone for you!" the pilot shouted.

Blue put it to his ear. "Hello?"

"Blue?" a voice said.

Blue smiled. "Howard. What are you doing up this late?"


\* \* \*

# CHAPTER FIVE

To the east, the sky turned pink, and then yellow.

The sun slowly rose over the dense green canopy of the forest, and the ribbons of dark water below. Mist rose from the river. A large white bird, a crane, left its hiding spot along the shoreline, and flapping its mighty wings, glided along the surface of the water.

Somewhere, a cock crowed, and further away, a dog howled in response. There were people living near here, though you would never guess it.

Nine crouched in the underbrush set back from a narrow, two-lane blacktop road. She had ditched the boat in the swamps sometime during the night. Then she had waded through standing water and across open land. Now she was here, and she was in trouble. Her battery was low. She didn't know if the water had gotten to it, or if Darryl's EMP had drained it, or if it was low for some other reason.

There was a red light blinking behind her eyes. She could see it there. It was an icon, shaped like an empty dry cell battery. It was annoying, first of all. But it was also a sign that she was running down. She needed to get somewhere so she could charge her battery back up. She didn't know where that would be. If she ran all the way down, she was sunk. Immortality was fraught with dangers - ones she had never considered.

And that wasn't the worst of it. The sky was busy with drones. She could see them up there, robots with mounted cameras, controlled from a remote location, buzzing around like giant insects. Some were high in the air, but a few were just above the tree line. They were looking for her.

If they spotted her, the best thing that could happen was they'd take a picture. But it wouldn't surprise her if the drones were armed. It wouldn't surprise her if they just blew her away. Clearly, that was the company's intention.

She stayed low in the bushes. Her mini-dress was soaked through. It clung to her body, leaving nothing to the imagination. In a way, it felt sexy. But this wasn't the time to feel sexy. Nor the place.

She still had Darryl's rifle. It had gotten wet, and she had no idea if it would fire now or not. There were limits to Susan's knowledge about guns. She did know that it had no sound suppressor, so if she did end up firing it, and if it worked, it was going to make a hell of a lot of noise.

She felt the possibilities narrowing for her. It was going to be very hard to escape from here. Daylight was coming. She was dressed for a wet t-shirt contest. Her battery was running down, and there was a ticking time bomb inside her. The drones were hunting her from the sky.

A car was coming.

She heard it before she saw it. It had the low rumble of a car with a big engine. Somewhere up this road, a car was cruising along, coming slow. She watched for it.

There were two choices: hide from it, or reveal herself. If it was a company car, then the game was over. If it was a civilian car, some passerby, then she was still alive for the time being. Darryl's face flashed across her databanks. It was his face as he lay dying in the bottom of the boat. She felt a pang of regret. Without knowing it, she had put Darryl in terrible danger. She would put the next person's life on the line knowing full well what she was doing.

Still, her instinct, like that of all living things, was to survive.

Here came the car. Her distance vision was exceptional, several times better than a human's. The car didn't look like a company car. It looked like a sports car. The emblem on the front grille was of a wild horse running.

She checked the sky. There were no black spots in sight, at least for the moment. She stepped out into the road. She put a long, sexy leg out, and her thumb. Her high breasts pressed forward, her nipples starkly visible against the thin, flimsy fabric of her soaked dress.

She kept the rifle draped along the back curve of her body, out of sight.

The car pulled up. It was a black Ford Mustang, a newer one, in excellent condition. The driver's window powered down. A man was at the wheel. He was ruggedly handsome, with deep blue eyes. He had a two-day growth of beard.

Nine recognized the type. He looked like a movie actor, or a man from a cigarette advertisement. She was designed to be attracted to all men and women, but some more than others. Her body naturally responded to people that others would find attractive. An electric current of excitement passed through her. She hoped it wouldn't drain her battery faster.

The man smiled. "Hello, beautiful," he said. "Need a ride?"

She nodded. "Yes."

He looked her body up and down. "Where to?" His smile became even broader. His teeth were white and perfectly straight.

In one fluid motion, she whipped the rifle around from behind her back and pointed it at his head. The barrel rested along her arm. Her finger rested on the trigger.

She smiled back. "Wherever you're going."

\* \* \*

Mr. Blue woke with a start.

He had been dreaming. His father was put away for good by the time Blue was eight years old. And his mother had taken on a string of bad boyfriends. One of them, Mel, was the last one. Mel used to beat Blue with his belt. But Blue was growing up. By the time he was fourteen, he was as big and tough as almost any man. Mel was too much of a drunk to get the memo.

Blue dreamed it exactly how he remembered it. Big Mel, with the bald head and the hairy chest, in his white sleeveless t-shirt, had come for Blue with the belt. Blue wrestled the belt away from him, and then he beat Mel down. Mel ended up on the floor, wedged in the over-sized space between the refrigerator and the wall.

Blue towered over him. "Get up," he said. "And get out of my house."

As the images faded from his mind, Blue could still hear his mom crying in the background. He blinked his eyes several times and shook his head.

It was morning. He was lying under the sheets of a king-sized platform bed. Bright sunlight streamed in through tall windows. On two sides of him, those windows gave him a sweeping view of the high-rise towers of downtown, as well as the harbor front. He was high above it all.

How long had he slept? Not long, maybe half an hour. Even that was too long. He was lucky to be alive, falling asleep like that.

They had given him a Suncoast corporate guest suite. When officials from the Pentagon came to town, these suites were where they slept. When corporate high-rollers flew in to buy fleets of the newest-generation Sexbots to hand out to their best people, this was where they stayed. The general managers of professional sports teams slept here, as did the special assistant to the Sultan of Brunei.

It wasn't a place where Blue usually slept. The company didn't often acknowledge their relationships with people like Blue. The Blues of this world were phantoms. They didn't exist. Suncoast didn't deal in espionage and murder. Suncoast most certainly did not murder its own employees.

All the same, Blue knew they didn't put him here as a reward. The job was a disaster. The story line was now outside their control. Suncoast liked to work in the dark. And suddenly, everything had exploded into the light.

Not good. Not what the company paid people like Blue for. They paid people like Blue to do things very quietly. In this case, that had failed. Now they were hiding him. Later today, they would whisk him to a private airstrip outside town, and fly him to a company compound in the Bahamas. After that, who knew? Wherever he wanted to go, or so they said.

Blue didn't believe a word of it. He reached under his pillow. His gun was there. It was a Glock, nine-millimeter, 17 shots in the magazine, fully-loaded. He had no idea if this gun would be enough to get him out of here.

A disturbing thought swam to the surface of Blue's mind. It wasn't the first time this particular thought had come to him. He was 45. He might be too old for this line of work. He'd been slow terminating Susan Jones yesterday. He had almost gotten killed twice himself.

Also, he had let Green get destroyed.

He smiled. He had never really liked Green. Talk about a robot with no personality? That was Green in a nutshell.

Even so, maybe it was time to retire. He had some money. He could buy a little beachfront shack on the Pacific Coast in Nicaragua, and spend his days selling ham sandwiches and beer to the surfers.

It sounded nice, but...

He rolled out of bed, nude, and padded with gun in hand to the doorway. He didn't have anything to wear. They had taken his jumpsuit from last night and were supposed to bring him some clothes this morning.

He pressed a button on the wall and the bedroom door slid open. He stepped into the doorway, but let his gun hand stay back behind the wall.

Three men stood in his living room. They were in a tight circle, whispering together. They looked up when Blue appeared. They seemed surprised to see him, or maybe embarrassed. Blue was the one who was nude, but they looked like they had been caught doing something they shouldn't.

Blue knew now why he had awakened. Even in sleep, he must have heard these guys come in. They were big guys, almost identical in bearing. Ex-high school athletes. They all wore sports jackets and slacks. They had crew cuts.

One of them was older, with a mustache. He was heavier set, his face lined with experience. He might even be Blue's age. He would be the one in charge.

"You guys have a change of clothes for me?" Blue said.

"Well," the boss said, and he smiled. It was a sheepish, shit-eating grin. "There's been a change of plans."

"Yeah? What's that?"

All three men raised guns.

Blue swung his gun around and fired it before the men got off a shot. One shot - he put a bullet right between the boss's eyes. A red dot of blood appeared on the guy's forehead. He stood still for one second, then dropped to the floor, dead before he hit the carpet.

Blue fired three times at the other guys, but they had already dived for cover. He missed all three shots. He ducked back into the bedroom.

A second later, a volley of return fire splintered the walls at the threshold. Blue backed away, waited a beat, then wrapped his gun hand around the doorway. He fired three more times.

He had already fired seven times. Seven shots down, ten to go. He took a deep breath. He needed to slow down for a second and think. If these guys called for back-up, he was finished. It was all on him. They could sit in the living room and wait him out. He was the one who had to get out of here.

A new volley of shots came, ripping up the doorway again. Blue dropped back. The shooting went on for a long time. Finally, it stopped.

He hesitated, but only for a second. Things could only get worse the longer he hung around this bedroom. If it was time to go, then it was time to go. He squatted, hearing his knees creak as he did, then he rolled into the living room. He came up on one knee.

A guy leaned against the side wall, like he was hiding. Not much cover there. Who were these guys? Blue put three bullets in him. The guy fell over, holding his guts. He disappeared behind a sofa. Blue fired three more shots through the sofa.

Thirteen shots down. Four to go.

The third guy was not here. Blue stood and walked over to the sofa. He glanced behind it. The guy he'd shot lay there, still alive, breathing heavily. His chest gave mighty heaves. He was shot through with holes. His suit was stained with blood. His teeth were gritted. He looked up at Blue.

"Listen," he said, gasping for breath.

"Sorry. No time for chatter today."

Blue shot him in the head. The skull popped apart, spraying blood and bone.

Now Blue glanced around. He had three shots left. He should crouch down and take this guy's gun, but he didn't dare do it. He had to finish the job first. He almost - almost - gave a thought to Howard. Treacherous Howard, who had sent these idiots in here to kill him. Blue supposed that the five million dollar payout for bringing back Number Nine was out of the question at this point.

Howard could wait.

Blue moved through the beautiful apartment, sleek, nude, gun out, in the shooter's stance he had learned in FBI training so long ago.

That guy had to be here somewhere.

Blue kicked in a bathroom door. Toilet, sink, glass shower. No one in there. He kept moving. He recognized how important time was.

He turned a corner.

A gun appeared from his right. He saw it in his peripheral vision, saw it and didn't really see it. He spun, too late.

The man had hidden in a tiny alcove. It was a good spot. He put the gun to Blue's head. Blue reached for it. He was half a second too late.

The man pulled the trigger.

Click.

Nothing happened.

It was a kid, maybe twenty-five years old. His face had barely seen a razor. His eyes were hard, but they were lying eyes.

The kid pulled the trigger again.

Click.

What was this, training day?

Blue shook his head, then pointed his own gun at the kid's face. The gun's muzzle was three inches from the kid's forehead.

The kid dropped his weapon.

"You see what happened here," Blue said, "is you got in a gunfight, but you didn't count your shots. You lost your head a little bit. So you ran out of bullets, and you didn't know it. You've had all this time hiding back here while I've been wandering around the apartment, and you could have reloaded. But you didn't."

He shrugged. "It's the kind of thing that comes with experience."

The kid smiled. "You don't want to give me another try, do you?"

Blue pulled the trigger, point blank range. The kid's face imploded. Blood and bone sprayed the white wall behind him. The kid's big body dropped to the floor. The bullet had put a whale of a ragged hole in the drywall.

"Nope," Blue said.

He padded back toward the living room. He had two shots left in his own gun. Pretty good for an old man. Still, if the kid had been thinking, Blue would be dead now. He was still alive because of luck.

He looked down at the boss man, the dead guy with the mustache. Sports jacket, slacks, dress shirt, leather loafers. He bent down near the body. That outfit looked like it might be a fit. What's more, the guy had dropped so quickly, he hadn't gotten blood on any of it.

"What do you run in jacket size?" he said to the dead man. "About a 48 long?"

\* \* \*

Howard sat in his living room, wrapped in a thick blue terrycloth robe. He felt like he was coming down with something, maybe a cold, maybe bronchitis. He was under a lot of stress.

It was a new day, and out his windows, the beach looked very, very inviting. Not that he was going to be on the beach today. It was aggravating. And it was all Blue's fault. Well, it was the last time Blue was going to fuck up, at least that much was certain. By now, Blue was either dead, or about to be.

The giant flat panel TV on the wall was on, showing advertisements during a break in the news. Howard was surrounded by people. Ed Morgan from public relations was here. He'd brought with him a woman, a consultant, Howard didn't know her name. He'd also brought a couple of his staff members. There were a couple of guys from the legal department. A guy from government relations. A couple of secretaries jotting down notes. Three Sexbots,

Howard's favorites, draped on various pieces of furniture.

There was too much chatter. A lot of people were talking at once. On the TV, a news woman came on. Below her face, little newsy updates were scrolling along from right to left.

*Missing scientist was Sexbot inventor...*

Howard raised a hand. "Can everybody shut the fuck up? Please?"

The chatter died down a bit, but there was still a low buzz.

"Shut up, I said."

"If you're just joining us," the anchorwoman said, "the big news this morning is a shootout during the overnight hours that left nine members of a security team from local corporation Suncoast Cybernetics dead. Details are sketchy at the moment, but the security detail was apparently sent to the North Port area home of this man, Darryl Blauer, a former United States Marine with two tours of duty in Afghanistan."

Blauer's face appeared on the screen. There were two images, a young Blauer in his Marine uniform, and a mugshot of an older, disfigured Blauer after an arrest.

"Blauer is the primary suspect in the disappearance of 33-year-old robotics scientist Susan Jones, who sources say may have been the inventor of the popular Sexbot line of robot sex toys. Sources say that Blauer, a Florida native and an expert backwoodsman, should be considered armed and extremely dangerous. He may be in possession of advanced, top-secret robotic equipment."

Howard threw his hands in the air. "Who are these sources? Have we said anything? We're the only source. I mean, for the love of God, people."

A photo of Susan appeared on the screen. Howard stared at it. She was in her cap and gown from her graduation at MIT. Howard had recruited her right out of school. She started working at Suncoast two weeks after that picture was taken. Howard felt something looking at that photo. He wasn't sure how he would describe the feeling.

He would like to talk to Susan again, if only one more time. She had been a nice girl once, and over the years, she really became kind of a raging bitch. It was like she thought she had built this company, and that she was the one who was somehow irreplaceable. She'd found out the hard way that it wasn't so.

"See, Susan?" he'd say to her. "I was the one who mattered."

On the screen, the focus shifted to a panel of experts.

"Suncoast says this is a simple sex toy," said a bald man in a speckled yellow bowtie. "But they're not convincing anyone. With all the explosions and the gunfights, there's talk starting about the military applications of some of these Suncoast robots."

"Notice how they suspect one of their scientists has been murdered, but they don't call the police," said a woman in a powder blue suit. "Instead, they send in their own security force. What are they hiding?"

"That's my point," said the bowtie man. "We're talking about a very secretive company here, which has sold more than a million sex toy robots worldwide in the past ten years, the highest-end models retailing for nearly $200,000 each."

The screen changed to a well-appointed living room full of Sexbots, standing and sitting in various states of undress, walking around, mingling with each other. Howard watched in disbelief. That scene was from an internal corporate video. Where did a TV station get their hands on that?

The bowtie man went on. "We're talking about billions of dollars in revenue. Plus those military contracts - no one knows the value of those, because the company won't share their client list or any contract details. But my sources tell me that Suncoast is one of the biggest suppliers of advanced robot soldiers to the Pentagon, for starters, and might also be selling robotics to third world dictators and possibly, Mexican drug cartels. This is a company that's becoming a law unto itself."

The chatter in the room erupted again. Howard felt a headache coming on.

"This is a nightmare," he said.

One of the public relations flacks, a fat young guy named Rob who was always sweaty and who looked like he was being choked to death by his own necktie, spoke up.

"Howard, I don't see what the big problem is here."

Howard shook his head. "What?"

Rob shrugged, the flesh of his neck jiggling. "I don't see the problem."

Howard took a deep breath.

"Let me see if I can explain it for you, Rob. The problem is we've got a missing scientist, nine dead security guards, and a rogue Sexbot that has apparently decided to start blowing things up all over town. And we have this in a very public way. Mr. and Mrs. Mainstream America don't like to hear about corporate armies with top secret technology while having their morning eye-opener. It gives them the tiniest hint at how far things have moved toward a world they might not like to live in."

Rob was undeterred. He waved a meaty hand. "Right. So let's give them a world they do want to live in. Listen, this is a great opportunity to change the conversation. Suncoast has too low a profile. I've been saying that for years. You can't buy this kind of media attention, Howard. I promise you, in the next week you're going to see a spike in sales like you've never seen. People are going to be talking about this company. You know what we need to come out with now? We need a Sexbot for the common man. Something that costs like, I don't know, five hundred or maybe a thousand dollars. Do we have anything like that in the works?"

Howard looked at him. "No."

Phones were ringing all over the room. A brown-haired Sexbot answered one of them, a classic old rotary-dial that sat on one of the end tables. "Howard, it's Councilman Mitchell's office," the Sexbot said. Her voice was so sultry that Howard longed for some alone time with her.

"Yeah, what do they want?"

"With all the media attention, they want to know if you're still having people over tonight." The Sexbot listened to the phone again. "The Masked Ball. Is it still on?"

Howard smiled. "Of course. We never cancel a party."

Another Sexbot, this one a curly blonde, came over and handed Howard a mobile phone. She didn't say anything as she handed it to him.

"Hello," he said.

"There was an accident," a voice said.

"Tell me," Howard said.

"The Blue Man," the voice said. Howard waited, expecting the next words to be: "He didn't make it."

But those weren't the next words. The next words that came were, "He left the building."

"What?" Howard said. "He left the building? What about the Three Wise Men?"

"They didn't make it."

Howard stared at the phone. Could it be right, the thing this person was saying? Had Blue just killed three company assassins? If it were true, it was the worst news he'd had all day. Mr. Blue roaming around in a good mood was bad enough. Blue out there in the world, whereabouts unknown, and in a bad mood? That was reason enough to declare a state of emergency.

"I'm sorry to hear that," Howard said.

"We were, too."

Howard hung up the phone.

All around him, people clamored for his attention. The room took on a surreal cast. He half-expected these people, his people, to begin removing the human masks from their faces, revealing mechanical clockworks beneath. They jabbered at him, their mouths huge, like the mouths of great white sharks, their teeth like the blades of an electric saw.

"Howard," they said.

"Howard... Howard... Howard."

He pulled his fuzzy robe tighter to his body. He gazed out the window at the sun-dappled ocean. Maybe he needed a vacation.

"Howard!"

\* \* \*

Blue stood on a busy street corner in downtown Sarasota, wearing the sports jacket, slacks, dress shirt and shoes of a recently deceased gunman. The clothes fit him okay. And the guy had decent taste. The jacket and the slacks were Brooks Brothers. The shoes were Italian loafers.

Nice.

Still, out in the open like this, Blue felt like he was wearing a big red target on his back. He half expected a bullet at any moment.

A taxi slowed down as it approached. Blue gave it a brief wave, and it pulled over to the curb. He slid into the back seat.

"Long Boat Key," he said to the driver, a man of vague Middle-eastern descent. Blue looked at the identification card on the back of the driver's seat. He didn't see anything there that suggested the driver was anybody but who he claimed to be.

"You like your work?" Blue said.

The driver shrugged, and pulled out into traffic. "Except for the old people in the big Cadillacs, I like it," the man said, with only a hint of an accent. Blue guessed that he'd come to the United States as a teenager. "They drive like it's bumper cars out here."

Blue took a deep breath and relaxed into the seat. This guy was a cab driver, nothing more, nothing less. Blue felt a little better now that he was off the street. He could take a moment to reflect.

The company had tried to kill him. That was bad. And by now, they knew he was still alive. They would come after him.

He could run. He had just over $500 in his pocket, also a gift from the dead man. The guy wouldn't need the money any more. Blue also had an account in Miami. It was a safe deposit box with tens of thousands of dollars in cash, plus a hundred thousand dollars in bearer bonds, and two new identities - social security cards, driver's licenses, the works. The key to the box was in an apartment in Miami Beach.

If he gave this cab driver the $500 in his pocket, and the promise of a thousand more when they got there, he was sure the man would drive him the 200 miles to Miami, then wait for him while he stepped inside the bank.

Yes, he could run. That would be the safest thing to do, his surest bet. He could be in Brazil, or Greece, or South Africa, in a day or two. He could lay low, let things blow over. Put a feeler out to Howard in a couple of months, see how the big dog was feeling about the whole thing.

On the other hand, the company had tried to kill him. Mr. Blue. After all he'd done for them? And in this case, it wasn't really the company. It was Howard. Howard had tried to kill Blue. You couldn't just let that float. You didn't run away from something like that. You ran right at it.

Also, there was this situation with Number Nine. Nine was almost certainly dead by now, and if she wasn't, the bomb would kill her tonight. But what if it didn't? What if at this time tomorrow, Nine was somehow still alive?

He and Number Nine had some unfinished business. He felt it. That little interaction in the motel was more than sexual. It was... explosive. Intense. She had murdered Green right in the middle of it. She had almost murdered Blue.

That made her a lot like Blue, didn't it? Ready for action. Ready for whatever came along. And in a sense, Mr. Blue had created Nine, hadn't he? The scientist would never have taken the chance to download herself if Blue hadn't come to murder her.

Blue hadn't murdered Susan Jones. Not really. He had given her a new, better life as Number Nine.

That sealed it. He would stay in town for now. He would go to Howard's party tonight, if it was still happening, and see what was shaking. If he could, he would find Nine. Hell, maybe he would capture her and sell her to the highest bidder. She was a live person inside a robot - that had to be worth real money. Then again, maybe he wouldn't sell her. Maybe he would... do something else with her.

In the meantime, outside of a few minutes shut-eye before this most recent shootout, he hadn't slept in nearly two days. He needed sleep, and a safe place to do it.

The cab cruised across the tall bridge to Longboat Key. Blue gazed out at the sky and the water. Now that he felt a little more relaxed, he could almost fall asleep in this car. Just close his eyes and let the motion rock him to sleep.

"Where are we going?" the cabbie said.

"Just drive," Blue said. "I'll know it when I see it."

\* \* \*

Nine stood inside the man's house.

It was a beautiful, modern, open design, split-level home. It stood on stilts above a stretch of waterway, surrounded by dense forest growth. The living room had huge windows, catching a southwest exposure and a view of a bend in the river. It was like living in a tree house.

She had brought him in here at gunpoint, but the man didn't seem to mind. She still held the rifle, but he was in his kitchen, puttering around with pots and pans. The burners were built into a counter that faced outward. The effect of it was he could cook and talk to her directly at the same time.

He wore blue jeans and a tight blue t-shirt that showed off his lean muscles. The shirt said YOGA MAN across the front. He wore sandals on his feet.

He looked across at her. "Can I interest you in some eggs?" he said. "Coffee?"

"That's okay," Nine said. "I don't..." What was she going to say? I don't eat? Yes, she had very nearly said that. Inside her eyes, the red battery light was blinking. It was going very fast. She was about to run down.

She felt tired. She hadn't slept at all last night. That shouldn't matter. She was a machine. She thought about the chimps, the ones inside the Sexbots in the monkey facility up in South Carolina. They would sleep. Maybe not like they once had, but they definitely slept. The machine didn't need it. The psyche did. That was the theory she and Martin had come up with.

"Would you like to take a shower?" the man said. "I promise I won't touch your gun."

She looked at the gun in her hand as if seeing it for the first time. It was a little embarrassing that she had held him at gunpoint.

"Sorry about that," she said. "I just..."

He raised a casual hand. "Don't worry about it. It happens to me once or twice a week. A beautiful girl wearing next to nothing flags me down on the road, then pulls out a machine gun. I'm used to it by now. Usually, they kidnap me, rather than bring me straight home."

Nine smiled. "Did anyone ever tell you that you look like a movie star?"

He shrugged. "The kidnappers do. That's generally why they kidnap me. They say I look like that Irish actor Colin Farrell. Most times, I end up letting them have their way with me."

Nine thought about it. Sure, Colin Farrell, that seemed about right. Shouldn't let it go his head, though.

"Do you need anything at all?" he said to her. "A sweater, some shoes, maybe a nuclear bomb?"

"Do you have a computer?" she said. "I need to check my email."

He gestured at a door across the living room from her. "In there. That's my little at-home office."

Nine headed for the room. She was running out of time.

"My name is Michael," the man called after her. "Do you have a name?"

She didn't turn around. "Believe me when I say you're better off not knowing it."

Inside the room, Nine found a laptop on a clear Lucite desk. The office itself was spare, with polished simulated wooden floors, and a sky light overhead. The desk platform was high off the ground, and there was no chair. This guy was one of those stand-up-at-work people. When Nine was Susan, she couldn't understand how they ever got any work done. Susan couldn't concentrate when standing.

But Nine didn't need to concentrate. What she needed was to recharge. The red light behind her eyes was going so fast, it was barely blinking any more. Once it went to solid red, she would have real trouble.

On her right forearm, up by her elbow, was a barely noticeable crevice about a quarter of an inch long. She stuck the thumbnail of her left hand into the crevice, and pulled. It took a moment, and a little more pressure than was comfortable, but she pried open a compartment that wasn't obviously there a moment before.

Inside was a black wire, coiled tight, with a USB plug at the end of it. She pulled the wire out and unwound it. She felt along the edges of the laptop until she found a USB port. She plugged herself in. It was rudimentary, but it would have to do.

A window appeared on the laptop screen.

There were numerous options she could choose. She could do a systems check. She could look at some usage data. She could reboot. She could re-charge. Indeed, the system was prompting her to re-charge.

"Power is critically low," it said in red letters. "Sexbot will power down soon to preserve system integrity. Click here to re-charge."

She clicked on re-charge. An empty progress bar appeared. A green field, which indicated power, was a tiny vertical slice all the way to the left. Gradually, as the system powered up, the green field would expand to the right, filling up the bar.

She planned to power up off this man's personal laptop, a unit better suited to juicing a portable music player. This was going to take a long time.

It might take all day to get to 50%. Then she had to deal with the bomb.

"I knew it was you," a voice said behind her.

Her gun was on the Lucite desk. With her left hand, she grabbed it, then spun halfway around. She pointed the gun at him. Michael. Her right arm was still attached to the computer.

He raised his hands, and his smile faltered for once.

"You knew it was who?" Nine said.

"Well, hear me out on this, okay? I promise I won't tell on you. I've had a lot of women come through this house, you know, kidnappers and such, but you're the first one to walk in here and plug herself into my laptop."

Nine stared at him. From the corner of her eye, she saw that the progress bar had moved the smallest amount. She might be juiced up to 3%. The red light behind her eyes blinked just a touch less intensely.

"I heard the explosions last night," Michael said. "It wasn't that far from here. When I checked the TV news this morning, you're all over it. They say an ex-Marine from back in the swamp murdered a scientist and stole a very high-tech Sexbot. On the internet, the conspiracy people are saying he stole a top-secret military robot. It looks to me like he stole a little of both."

"He didn't steal anything," Nine said. "He's being framed. And anyway, he's dead."

She saw the look in his eyes, and shook her head. "They killed him. The company. I didn't do it."

"Are you running from them?" he said.

She nodded.

He nodded, too. His lips found the ghost of a smile again. "Okay. Well, listen. As I said, my name is Michael. And you can call me Michael. Not Mike, not Mikey. Michael. Okay? I'll do whatever I can to protect you. If you don't want to go back, you don't have to. You can stay here as long as you like. I've got some motor oil if you want something to drink. I've also got some old fiber optic cabling you can chew on. Do you have a name?"

"They call me Nine," she said. "Number Nine." It was a nice gesture he was making. But Nine knew that when the time came, this man Michael wouldn't have much say in whether she stayed or went. And if the company came, there really wasn't a whole lot he could do to protect her.

"Number Nine?" he said. "That's not much of a name, is it?" He pointed at the laptop. "Is that you powering up? You're never going to do it like that. My other car is an electric. It's fancy. I have the repair bills to prove it. And I have a home juicing station downstairs in the garage. Actually, I've also got a little portable one that I take on trips. I can bring it upstairs, and you can plug in right here in total comfort. I'll bet I can fill you up in record time."

She smiled. She looked him up and down, the way men sometimes did to women. She liked what she saw.

"I'll bet you can, too."

\* \* \*

Howard was on the phone, taking the one call he dreaded the most.

Everyone had finally cleared out of his living room. Everyone but the Sexbots. In a little while, he would carve out some time to spend with them. God, he was stressed out. He needed some relaxation of the kind that only his girls could provide.

"Howard?" the Chairman said over the line.

"Yes, sir."

Howard shook his head. The Chairman. James Walsh. What a clown. He was older than dirt. He was up in New York, snowed in, gazing at printouts from his ten billion dollar portfolio. He was a money manager, a stock market swindler, and a hostile takeover king. He didn't know how to run a real company. He should leave Suncoast to the experts.

Howard stared out at the ocean as the Chairman deployed one of his favorite weapons, the pregnant pause. Howard wouldn't stand for it, though. He knew how to beat it. The trick was to detach. He started counting silently, down from ten to one.

"Howard."

"Yes. I'm here."

"Howard, what the fuck is going on down there?"

"Sir?"

"Don't play dumb with me, Howard. Last night, I received a phone call. It led me to believe that everything was going according to plan."

"Yes. I received the same phone call, sir."

"So what happened? I see on the news this morning that in fact, everything is not going according to plan."

"We're still trying to figure that out, sir." Howard hated that word coming out of his mouth. Sir. Sir. Why did he always call this bastard sir?

"You're trying to figure it out? Let me tell you something, Howard. I don't believe a word you're saying. Who sent that team in there last night, if not you? Why did you send them? You blew up a man's house, for the love of Christ. Don't tell me you're trying to figure it out. Why did you do it? You must have a reason."

Howard motioned for one of the Sexbots, the black one, the one he called Jezebel, to come over. He also motioned to one of the blondes, Cassandra. This conversation was going poorly. He needed to relax, and he needed to relax now.

"Well sir, there's some concern that Susan, ah, how to put this…"

"Just spit it out, Howard. Before I find someone else to run that company."

Jezebel arrived, followed soon after by Cassandra. Gently, Howard pushed them to their knees. It didn't take much. They knew the drill very well. With one hand, he pulled the knot on his bathrobe's soft belt. The bathrobe fell open, revealing Howard in all his glory. The two girls went to work on him, faces pressed very close together. Now that would make a pretty picture.

He took a deep breath. Boy, he was starting to feel better already.

"It seems that Susan, before she was terminated, might have…"

"Yes?"

Howard put a proprietary hand on Cassandra's head. He was erect now. Very, very erect. The two girls kissed, his member hard between them. He was proud - very proud - of these girls. He was proud of himself.

"Well, she might have been able to download herself into the unit she kept there at her house."

"She what? Howard, did I hear you…"

"Yes."

"Jesus."

Howard watched his girls. Very nice. He took a deep, deep breath.

"It was completely unsanctioned," he said, feeling calmer now. "And it was done in an uncontrolled environment. As far as we know, the operating system on the unit wasn't erased, which is obviously not our intention going forward. We don't want real people living inside sex toys, as you know. So it's possible that..."

"Where is she?" the Chairman said.

Howard was having trouble concentrating. Things were building, becoming heightened.

"Eh, we're looking for her."

"So you don't know where she is?"

"That's correct, sir."

He found that the word sir didn't taste so bad right now. Not nearly so bad. He gazed down at the two heads, black hair, blonde hair, moving in unison. It was crazy. He was talking to the Chairman!

Fuck the Chairman.

Hooray!

"Listen to me, Howard. I built this company. Not you. You were an undergrad when I bought a company that made pool cleaners. They are dragging our good name through the mud. On TV, right now, all day. CNN, MSNBC, all the rest. We are in the 24-hour news cycle, Howard. I won't stand for it. If that robot falls into the wrong hands, the police, the courts, some do-gooder group, things will only get worse for us. It will become very hard to move forward with our immediate plans. Those plans are..." For once, the Chairman's voice faltered. "They're very important to me."

"I know," Howard said.

"I want you to destroy the robot," the Chairman said. "Do you understand? I want it found and destroyed by tonight."

"Yes. I understand."

It was funny. Howard did understand. But now, with the girls at his feet like this, and the dying Chairman pulling his hair out over the phone, a new thought occurred to Howard. There was another way to play this.

"No one is irreplaceable, Howard. You need to understand that. You're in a very vulnerable position. This isn't the kind of job you just retire from, Howard. There's too much on the line."

Howard smiled. What was the Chairman hinting at? That he would have Howard killed? My, my, my. Did he really want to go there? Blue wasn't the only incredibly lethal killer that Howard had access to, not by a long shot.

Anyway, never mind all that. Howard preferred to think about Susan right now. A thought about her had come to him.

Back in those early days, he had tried to date Susan. It was true. In the days before Sexbots, he had asked her out a few times. Was that inappropriate for a boss to ask out an employee? He didn't know. He didn't care. At this point, Howard hadn't asked a flesh and blood woman out in years. But back then? Yes, he had dated women.

Susan was too haughty. She always said no. She was too full of herself, and her great future as a scientist. She was too busy working, trying to make breakthroughs, to give Howard the time of day. But look at her now. She was dead, trapped inside a sex toy, and on the run. Where had that great future gone?

He found that he did want to see her again, if only one more time. He took another deep breath.

Over the phone, the Chairman raged on. He seemed far away. *Steady, old boy, don't give yourself a stroke. The cancer will kill you soon enough.*

Howard looked down at his girls again. They were really working him. They licked him. They kissed and licked each other. He couldn't watch them. It was too much. They would finish him off too fast. He looked out at the ocean again.

God. What a day. He skated along the edge of a climax. Howard thought about Susan, trapped inside Number Nine, and how if he could, he would bring her here. And he would have her, just like he had these girls.

And when it was over, when he'd had her in every way he wanted her, in every way possible, he would say, "Look at you now, Susan. Look at the great scientist. My little slave."

And that thought, the thought of Susan on her knees here like these girls, made Howard explode.

\* \* \*

Nine was juiced.

It was late morning. The charge had taken a long while, but the blinking red light was gone. It was now replaced by a warm green glow. The green must have always been there before the red blinking started, but she never noticed it. It wasn't distracting like the red light. It wasn't visible in the same way. It was more like the glow of health, and it filled up her senses.

There was trouble ahead, she knew that. The company was after her. There was a bomb counting down inside her. Just over ten hours left. But she didn't want to think of those things. She wanted to relax for the moment, and enjoy this feeling.

She sat on the sofa in Michael's living room, still plugged into his portable black re-charger. Sunlight streamed through the windows, reflected off the green water that flowed by below. Looking out that window, if someone didn't know better, they might think they were in Africa.

Michael ate his breakfast at the table across the room from her. His beard was well-groomed. His hair was just so. He seemed relaxed, completely at home in his body.

He smiled when he looked at her. That was when the movie star looks came out the most. Nine recognized a feeling rising in herself. Desire. She deduced that the more power she had coursing through her system, the more her dominant programming would come to the fore.

In other words, Number Nine was getting horny.

"I'm fascinated by you," Michael said. "I mean, you're a machine, right? But you're also a lot like a person. If I met you in different circumstances…"

"Like, if I didn't step out of the woods and pull a gun on you?"

"Right. Let's say we were at a party, a fancy dress-up affair, and the host was making introductions, and we took each other's hands, you know? And we looked deep into each other's eyes. And I said, 'Hi, I'm Michael.' And you said, 'Hi, I'm Nine.'"

He raised a hand, as if to say STOP.

"You know, you'd probably have a name instead of a number. I mean, where is this party, at the factory? Who has a number instead of a name? So let's give you a name. How about Rachel?"

Nine smiled. She was willing to play along.

"So if you said, 'Hi, I'm Rachel,' I'd never guess you were a robot. I'd just think you were a beautiful woman that I was lucky to meet at a party."

He got up from the table, and came across the room toward her. He looked at her very intensely.

"What's it like?" he said.

"What's what like?"

He shrugged. "To be what you are. To be who you are. You're obviously so advanced, so smart, that it must be strange. What's it like in there?"

"I think it's probably not much different from being inside you," she said. "I mean, how do you know you're not like me?"

He shook his head. "I don't. But... I eat food, right?"

"Right. But what is food?"

She stood up from the sofa.

He came close and faced her. "I know. It's just that..."

Nine turned away from him. Rachel. It was such a nice name. She remembered how she was Susan. And how Susan was always busy with work, always busy becoming something great, that her parents could be proud of, that she could be proud of.

But Susan, at bottom, had been lonely. She had never been beautiful. And she had been very, very smart. It was a bad combination.

She was lying to herself, wasn't she? Lack of beauty hadn't been the problem. Beauty was as much a curse as a blessing. Nine was beautiful, and she got a lot of attention from killers and maniacs.

No. Susan's loneliness had been her own fault. She would never let a man get close to her. Since she finished college, the only one was Martin, but they were scientists together. They were pals. They were partners in a great discovery. And afterwards, she had pushed him away.

"The re-charge is almost done," she said. "It's at 98%. It probably won't top up. You know, the first 95% takes half the time, and the last 5% takes the other half."

Michael touched her shoulder. Movie-star handsome Michael.

She turned back to say something, but never remembered what she intended to say because suddenly he was there, and his lips settled against hers. She felt the damp sweep of his tongue across them. Uttering a soft whimper, she moved closer to him. Her breasts were flattened against his chest. Their thighs came together.

"Michael…"

"Lovely Rachel. I've wanted you since I first saw you."

"Gun in hand?" she said.

"Yes, the gun was very sexy."

Rubbing her lips apart with his, he pushed his tongue deep into her mouth. She moaned with hunger. His hands moved to her waist and pulled her more firmly against him. He cupped the round curve of her bottom and held her against the front of his body while they kissed deeply.

She clutched at him and responded to the hungry thrusts of his tongue. He released her long enough to pull his t-shirt over his head. He undid his belt and pulled the buttons of his jeans open, then gathered her against him again.

He caressed her breasts through the insubstantial material of her mini-dress. Dissatisfied with that, he released her spaghetti straps.

Nine gave a soft, ecstatic cry when her hot, flushed breasts met the warm solidity of his chest. Michael released a low, tortured groan. He pushed the dress past her hips until it slid down her thighs to the floor.

She pushed him backwards, toward the sofa. He sat down, and pulled his jeans down to his feet, struggling to kick free of them. For a moment, she hesitated. She hadn't been with a man with this way since... forever.

She kicked a leg over him, and lowered herself onto him. She sat astride his lap, facing him. They looked into each other's eyes.

"I wanted you, too," she said.

She closed her arms around his head, hugging it tightly against her, while she pressed her hips down onto his thighs, driving deep inside her. She moved against him, and he began to move inside her, advancing and retreating. She bounced on him, harder, harder. She rode him. She threw her head back. Her body shuddered.

"Yes!" she heard herself cry.

* * *

She and Michael were in his bed.

His bed was a king-sized, and it faced out toward the river. Hours had passed, and the daylight was growing short.

They were both nude from earlier. Nine had slept, and now she was awake. She didn't remember sleeping, and she didn't remember waking.

He was next to her, on her right side, exploring her body. His fingers moved along slowly, very experienced fingers, in danger of turning her on again. Sex with Michael had been something of a revelation. They had done it seven times, over and over, a marathon. It was fun, with no baggage of any kind, just two beautiful bodies coming together again and again. And again.

And again.

She thought of the last time she'd had sex before today. It was the day when she and Martin were first able to transfer a chimpanzee to a Sexbot, about nine months ago at the primate research facility outside Charleston, South Carolina. Afterward, the two of them had celebrated with drinks at the hotel bar. They got very drunk that night, and she went back to Martin's room with him.

In the morning, she had regretted it. Badly hung over, she regretted everything.

"We made a mistake," she said as she put her clothes on.

"By sleeping together?" Martin said. "I don't think so. I think it's great."

"All of it," she said. "The apes we're experimenting on. The two of us in here celebrating our great triumph. It's a disaster. It's a... it's a sin."

She looked at Martin in the mirror. He was lying in bed, propped up on a mountain of pillows, with his hands on top of his head. Easygoing, boy genius, ever-optimistic Martin. He looked so much like her dad. He smiled.

"Come on. Lighten up. There's no such thing as sin."

"I'm afraid," she said. "We opened Pandora's box, and there's going to be a price to pay." And of course, the punishment had finally come. Martin was dead and she was as much a guinea pig as any of the chimps.

Now, in Michael's bed, she shook her head to clear the memory. "Did I sleep much?" she said.

Michael smiled. "Sleep? You slept all day. I didn't even know that you could sleep. But yeah, you slept all right. You slept like the dead. To be fair, I slept too."

His hands felt good on her skin. They were big, strong hands. He traced the curve of her torso until his fingers reached the keypad and digital readout attached under her arm. He touched it, made a gentle circle around it.

A feeling of dread went through her. She would almost say she felt sick to her stomach.

"What is this thing?" Michael said. "I noticed it before. It's the only part of you that doesn't seem like a real woman."

Nine took a deep breath. "What does it say on it?"

"Well, it seems to be a countdown of some sort. Right now, it says three hours, thirty-seven minutes, with the seconds just flying by."

She nodded. "That's exactly what it is. It's a counter, and it's attached to a bomb that's somewhere inside me."

He looked at her sharply. "What?"

"Yes. I have a bomb inside me. When the countdown reaches zero, I think I'm going to explode."

He put a hand to his head. "Why would someone put a bomb inside you?"

Her lips started to tremble. "In case I escaped."

Suddenly she was crying. She didn't expect it to happen. She had felt perfectly stable until just a moment ago. She didn't even think she still had emotions. But then everything welled up inside her, and she wept in grief and terror. She was crying and he held her against his chest.

"What a waste," she said. Her body was wracked by sobs, and she could no longer speak. Michael didn't say anything. He just held her tighter.

Her life! The big scientific superstar. She had been so driven to succeed, to make her mark, and instead she ended up making sex toys for rich perverts, then torturing chimpanzees and putting their minds inside machines. Now the same thing had happened to her, and pretty soon, in just about five hours, she was going to die.

"It's okay," Michael cooed softly. "It's okay."

She would stay here, if there were any choice. She would stay for a night, or a week, or a month. She would let all of this pass her by. It was a beautiful home, and a beautiful man. She would stay here and make love to Michael, and watch the river, and notice every day how the sunlight came through the windows and the skylights. It made for a nice fantasy, but it wasn't to be. Her life was over. She had reached the end.

At some point, she noticed Michael's bare chest was heaving. She looked at his face, and he was crying too.

"I can't help it," he said. "I don't want you to die. It's not fair."

She took a deep breath. "I know," she said.

"If I cut you open," he said, "would it hurt?"

She shook her head. "Not really. Not like it would hurt you. Why?"

"Maybe I can cut the bomb out."

"Michael, do you know anything about bombs? Or about technology?"

He smiled, but it was a smile with no humor in it. His eyes were red. "I'm a quick learner. I'm a builder, and I have tools. I've looked at electrical systems before. I could get in there, and just... I don't know. Take a poke around. I'll go slow, not touch anything right away. Maybe it would be obvious what to do."

"Michael, shhhhh. Let's just..."

She moved up and pushed her face against his. Their cheeks touched. Their tears mingled like rainwater. She hugged him tightly, and he hugged her back. They stayed that way for a long time, just pressing together. For Nine, sometimes the crying was powerful, her whole body shaking with the force of her sobs. At other times, the crying was softer, almost subsiding completely.

Gradually, as they lay there pressed against each other, she became aware that Michael had an erection. Soon, she was ready too, maybe from all the emotion, maybe from just having him there. She reached down with one hand and gently guided him inside her. Then they lay still, their bodies perfectly entwined, joined, no space between them.

She pressed harder against him. She felt almost like she wanted to become him, their chests and legs melting until they became one person. She held the back of his head with her hand. He was crying again, and the feeling of it was contagious, because she began to cry again, too. And their mouths found each other. They kissed passionately, bodies moving gently, tears streaming down their faces. It went on a long time.

Afterward, she was lying in bed.

She must have fallen asleep again, because Michael wasn't in bed with her, and she didn't remember him getting up. For the moment, she felt good. She felt refreshed. She felt almost at peace.

This was a great big, comfortable bed, and it was amazing to simply be in it. It was luxurious, and Nine's programming made her very aware, and appreciative, of luxuries. She was relaxed enough to reflect on things.

Maybe there was room for hope. She had tried to put the bomb out of her mind, to wish it away, but now she allowed herself to think about it. Maybe Michael could open her up, and somehow disable it. He was smart. There might be instructions about it online. There might be an expert he could call, who would walk him through the process. She glanced at the clock on the bedside table. It was 7:15. There were just under three hours left, not much time, but maybe enough.

She had been here at Michael's since this morning, and now it was nearly nightfall. For a second, she wondered if the storm hadn't passed. She had no GPS unit installed. She had no remote access capability. The company had no way to find her.

What if she stayed hidden here? She pictured it in her mind. Just living here quietly, being partners with Michael. It wouldn't last forever. She knew that. But he could help her. He said he would. Maybe she could get a new identity, forged papers. When the time came, she could leave the country.

Her first priority would be contacting her parents. She couldn't do it directly. They'd have trouble believing her story, and anyway, they were probably being monitored. But how long would the company monitor them? Maybe not that long. Not forever, certainly.

In a few days, if they didn't find her, the company would assume she had died. They had probably found Darryl's body by now. Sooner or later, they were just going to decide that the bomb had gone off, or that she was rotting away at the bottom of one of the swamps.

The company wasn't all powerful. They couldn't...

The doorbell rang. It filled the house with a musical chime, which echoed from room to room. For all the effect it had, it might as well be an air raid siren.

\* \* \*

# CHAPTER SIX

Michael stood at his kitchen counter.

He was digging through a toolbox and inspecting various cutting devices when the doorbell rang. At first, he ignored it. He lived pretty far out. The only people who ever came to his door were Jehovah's Witnesses and Mormons. Michael wasn't into religion. And he had other, more pressing matters on his mind.

"Go away religious fanatics," he said under his breath.

He could do this. He could save Rachel. At first, it would be like cutting through something that sure felt like human skin. He would just have to keep in mind that she wasn't human, and she wouldn't really feel the pain. He doubted there would be anything like blood or gore. After the flesh, there was probably a layer of metal or hard plastic. He would just follow whatever metal line or wiring extended down from the digital readout on the surface. Then he would...

The doorbell rang again.

"Persistent, aren't we?"

When Michael opened the door, two men in dark blue uniforms stood on his front porch. They didn't look like soul savers or Bible salesmen. They looked like soldiers. They were young, big and muscular, with closely cropped hair. Their eyes were flat and blank. They each had an insignia on their chests, which looked to Michael like an eye peering over a desk. Their uniforms puffed out slightly, as if they had an umpire's padding under there.

Michael knew enough. They were wearing body armor.

Flat black guns were holstered at their waists.

One of them held a computer tablet in a big, thick hand. He referred to it, then looked up.

"Michael Simms?" he said.

Michael ran a hand through his hair. He sniffed slightly, as if he were tired, or maybe a little under the weather. He was painfully aware of his own fit, but thin body, his silly YOGA MAN shirt, his washed out jeans, and his bare feet. He had no military training. He hadn't been in a fight since the fourth grade. The truth was, he had gotten by for much of his life on looks, and brains, and charm.

Charm wouldn't persuade these men of anything. Michael was suddenly sorry he had opened the door. He stifled an urge to turn around and see what Rachel was doing back in the house.

It had been a beautiful day, the best in a long, long while. Then the bomb. And now this.

"Michael Simms?" the man said again.

"And you are?" Michael said.

"We're doing a security check of the neighborhood. There was an incident last night you may have heard about. Now there's a woman on the loose who is extremely dangerous. She was last seen not far from here. Do you know anything about this?"

Michael shrugged. Lying wasn't really part of his skill set. He shook his head. "I have no idea. I haven't noticed anything, but I've been asleep all day. I just got up. I was working late last night."

"What do you do?" the soldier said. His flat eyes stared at Michael. Now Michael was very, very sorry he opened the door.

"Uh, I'm a bartender. I work sometimes at the Ritz-Carlton

hotel bar downtown."

The two of them, they were both staring at him.

"Listen, who are you guys?"

"You haven't seen anything out of the ordinary?"

"I told you," Michael said. "I was asleep."

"Okay sir. Thank you for your time."

The two men turned, almost in unison, and walked down the stairs. Michael looked, and for the first time noticed their black Jeep parked in his driveway circle. As they climbed in, they turned and stared at him. One of them pointed a finger at him like it was an imaginary gun. Then he smiled.

Michael went inside, closed the door and locked it. He slid the deadbolt. He went into the bedroom, but Rachel wasn't there. He turned to his left, and there she was in a low crouch against the wall, nude, pointing her big rifle at the doorway.

At him. At Michael.

"Who were they?" she said.

"I don't know. They said they were some kind of security."

"Did they ask about me?"

"Yes."

"What did you tell them?"

"Rachel, look…"

She shook her head. "My name is Nine. What did you tell them?"

"I told them I was asleep all day. That I work nights as a bartender."

"Do you?"

"Do I what?"

"Do you work nights as a bartender?"

"No. Well, I used to. About 15 years ago."

She let her head sink to the wooden floor. "Oh Jesus, Michael."

* * *

Howard got the call on his encrypted line.

He didn't know the voice he was talking to. It was a kid, but the kid sounded competent enough. They'd been going house to house all day, and they had stumbled upon something. It looked like they had found her.

"Where is she?" Howard said.

"Inside a house, about five miles as the crow flies from where she was last seen. The house is only three miles from where we found the airboat with Darryl Blauer's body."

"How sure are we that this is it?"

"99%."

"Anybody in there with her?"

"A guy, Michael Simms, 38 years old. That's how we know we have the right place. He told our men he was asleep all day because he works nights. He said he was a bartender at the Ritz-Carlton. It doesn't check out. He was lying. He's a master carpenter. House builder. Get this, he builds eco-houses. Recycled materials. Solar power. That kind of thing. He hasn't been a bartender since he was 23."

Howard liked it. He liked the sound of this Michael Simms. He liked tree huggers. In general, you could run right over them.

"Military service?" he said.

"None."

Even better. This guy was no Darryl Blauer, a man who would rather die than give them back their own property. A man they should have seen coming. If Blue had been a little more on the ball, they would have.

The thought of Blue gave Howard a moment of pause. He gazed out the window. The last pink and purple sliver of sunlight was fading from the sky. The ocean looked like a bruise. Blue was out there somewhere, hopefully running for his life.

"Weapons registered to him?" Howard said. "I don't want any

repeats of last night."

"None."

"That doesn't mean he doesn't have any. Don't get cocky."

"Yes, sir. We'll be careful."

"Good. Then take her. Blow the door down. Blow the walls out. Blow the house to kingdom come. Whatever it takes. Just don't damage the Sexbot. I want it taken fully functional. Got that?"

"Sir, last night the orders were…"

"Last night was last night. It didn't go very well last night, did it? So the orders have changed. I want the Sexbot. I want it brought here to my house. And I want it undamaged. It's a very expensive and very sensitive piece of equipment. Are we clear?"

"We're clear. What about the guy? Michael Simms?"

Howard shook his head. "He's dead. It's very sad, but she already killed him before we got there. There was nothing we could do. See what I mean?"

"Uh, what about the press? Another death and it could look…"

"Damn the press," Howard said. "That's not your job. You let me worry about that. Just do what I tell you and get it done."

"Yes, sir."

Howard hung up the phone. Outside the window, night was here, black as smoke. He could see his reflection in the floor-to-ceiling glass that just a moment ago showed him the ocean. Two lovely Sexbots, dressed in sheer teddies, lounged on the furniture behind him. He smiled at himself. He was throwing a party tonight, and it was going to be fun. Only very special people were invited. And, as always, there were going to be pictures taken of all his guests, pictures that would come in handy in the months and years ahead.

Howard ran a tight ship. The sky was the limit for this company, and for Howard himself. For a second, he imagined a scenario where the President of the United States came to one of his parties and indulged himself. He imagined having photos of the President in naked repose with a few of the company's most charming ladies.

It was a fleeting image, fading very quickly. One step at a time, he told himself. One step at a time.

He thought of that company soldier on the phone just now, and he smiled again, even broader than before. He liked it when other people had to call him sir for a change. There was more of that coming in the future.

"Girls," he said to the two Sexbots. "Let's get ready for the party, shall we?"

\* \* \*

Nine was up and moving. There wasn't much time.

"Do you have any women's clothes around here?" she said to Michael.

He looked sheepish. He couldn't meet her eyes. He gestured at a walk-in closet. "On the right side. I had someone living with me for a while last year. One day she left. I've kept her clothes, thinking she might come back for them. So far, she hasn't."

Nine went in there. Slinky dresses and lingerie. High heels. A pair of blue jeans. No good. She didn't like jeans. Then she found a mostly sheer, skin-colored body stocking. That looked good. She put her feet in it and pulled it on over her body. It felt good. It felt right. It was sexy. It clung to her curves.

On the floor she found a pair of bright orange sneakers. Size 8 women's. They fit. Each sneaker had a balled-up ankle-height running sock in it. It seemed that this woman had left abruptly. Just as Nine was about to do.

She sat on the floor and pulled on the socks and sneakers. Then she jumped up and bounced in them a couple of times. They felt good. In case she had to run, she had the right shoes for it.

She walked out of the closet.

Michael's eyes lit up when he saw her. "Wow. You look…"

She went to the gun on the table and picked it up. "Do you have a gun?"

He shook his head. "Me? No. It's not my thing."

She turned back to him. He was cute. There was no sense denying it. He was an awesome lover. He was God's gift to the female race. It occurred to her that was probably why the body stocking lady had left so suddenly. When you're God's gift, you have to share it around. Not everyone is comfortable with that.

"I need to take my gun. I can't leave it with you. Sorry about that. I also need to borrow your car."

He raised an eyebrow. "The electric?"

She shook her head. "The Mustang. I need something that can go."

"Hey, listen…"

She pointed the gun at him. She stuck her other hand out. "Keys."

He stared at her. "Would you do it? Would you really shoot me? After we…"

"Michael, I like you very much. But I'm running out of time. Those men are coming back, and when they do, if I'm still here, you're going to be very sorry. They won't hesitate to shoot you. Whether I do it, or they do it, doesn't really matter. So don't test me, okay?"

He reached into the drawer of a small end table, picked up a set of keys, and put them in her hand. "That's an expensive car. It's my baby."

She smiled. "I'll be careful with it."

"I hope so."

She began to think through his options. "When I leave, they'll come back for you. They're not cops. They're corporate security. Some of them are hired killers. If they find you here, they'll probably kill you and say I did it. I think your best hope is to call 9-1-1, tell them I held you hostage, and that I just stole your car. Make it clear that I'm no longer here, but you're still alive and in danger. You need an ambulance. You're having a heart attack. Something like that. Do you have an attic?"

"I have a crawl space."

"Is there a window?"

"A small one."

"Can you fit through it?"

He smiled. "I don't know. I haven't tried."

"Michael..."

He shrugged. "Yeah. I could squeeze through it if I had to."

She nodded. "Okay. Good. Make sure all the doors are locked down here, then hide in the crawl space until the cops or an ambulance comes. The doors probably won't matter, they'll just blow them off the hinges, but it might buy you a few extra seconds. Don't come out for any reason until you hear sirens approaching. Even then, wait for them to find you. If the house catches fire, crawl through the window and climb down to the ground."

Michael just stared at her, his mouth slightly open.

"Okay?" she said.

"Why can't I just come with you?"

She shook her head. "I wish you could, I'd like to keep you, but if you come with me, you'll be dead inside three minutes. Really, this is the best way."

"How will you survive?" he said. "You're not a soldier. You're not designed for battle."

"Michael, do I really need to give you the stats? No, I'm not designed for battle. But put it this way. I'm 98% charged. At a full charge, I'm five times stronger than you. I can run three times as fast. My vision is like an eagle's. My hearing is vastly better. So are my reflexes. I'm a technology expert, and I can shoot a man's eye out at 25 yards. Those last two aren't factory specs, but let's just say they're add-ons from my original designer. Plus, I could be pierced by ten bullets, and if none of them cut my wiring or hit my hard drive

SEXBOT

- which is wrapped in case-hardened steel, by the way - then I'll just keep going."

She tapped his skull. "You, on the other hand. One bullet here, and you're finished."

"What about the bomb?" he said.

"I don't know. Something might turn up. Maybe I'll get lucky."

He shrugged. "Okay. You win."

She shook her head. "Believe me. I don't win. There's almost no possible scenario here where I don't lose."

He moved closer to her. They embraced. She felt his body against her sheer body suit. Immediately, the heat began to rise between them.

"I would have stayed," she said.

He looked in her eyes. "I know. I would have liked that." He paused, and his eyes lit up at an idea. "If you make it..."

She smiled. "Sure. But I wouldn't wait up if I were you."

He took her face in his hands, and they kissed, long and deep.

"I had a great day," he said.

"So did I. It was the best sexual experience I've ever had. I mean that."

"Coming from you..."

"You might be surprised."

He pulled away and looked at her. She shook her head now. "No sense wondering, Michael. I've got to go. I'll come back one day, if I can. I hope you're still alive."

"Thanks. I appreciate that."

Nine turned, gun in hand, went down the staircase to the basement workshop, and walked through to the garage.

* * *

The sun had gone down. Night was here.

The assault team closed in.

Twenty men came in five armored SUVs. Eight men approached from the front, five through the woods on either flank. Two men, the team leaders, hung back at the cars as a viewing and command post. There was an airboat on the creek behind the house, with one driver and two sharpshooters on board.

The men all wore Kevlar body suits and helmets. The company had learned its lesson the night before. There would be no mistakes this time.

Four men crossed quietly in front of the two car garage. The lead man carried a thirty-pound steel battering ram, which should take the front door out in one or two swings. Each man after that had a flashbang stun grenade. Each man carried a shotgun. The plan was to blow the front door, then throw the flashbangs in. If the team was lucky, the blasts and the blinding light might disable the subjects, or might get them running to the back porch, where the snipers would take them out.

On the other hand, it might make them hole up, spoiling for a fight. The third man in line, a young guy named Kevin, wiped some sweat out of his eyes. It was another steamy evening. Truth be told, he was nervous.

He'd heard about how it went the night before. Nine men dead, seven injured, two in critical. He didn't want to die, not for a job. He had spent four years in the U.S. Army, two full tours overseas, and he was willing to die for his country. But for a company that made sex toys? It seemed like a stretch.

He had a feeling in his bowels, a loose feeling like how it was before he went into a firefight. He could easily shit his pants. He smiled. Loose bowels were his good luck charm. He'd never gotten so much as a scratch in combat.

*Stop it. Pay attention.*

He brought his mind back to the present moment. The line of men leaned up against the garage door. The stairs were a right turn ten feet ahead. This had to happen fast. He pictured it in his mind.

BAM! The door came down, and they threw their flash bangs. His would be second. Fall back, wait for the explosions, then rush in.

Somewhere nearby, there was a sound.

It was muffled, but it sounded like a powerful car engine. And it sounded like it was right on the other side of this garage door.

The guy in front of him looked back at Kevin. His eyes widened. They both turned and looked at the door.

\* \* \*

Nine wasn't fully-charged. She was turbo-charged.

She sat in the driver's seat of the Mustang inside Michael's closed garage. Parked next to her was the electric car, but she barely noticed it.

She had her gun, lying across the seat next to her. Her hands gripped the steering wheel. It was silent in here, but on the other side of the garage door, she could hear the men massing as they approached the house. A vehicle pulled up. Another. Another. They sounded like trucks.

Men were speaking in hushed tones. Someone was giving orders. The voices were too low for her to make out what was said. It was time, though. They were here for her, and it was time for her to go.

She turned the key in the ignition and the engine barked into life. There was no turning back now. She had a clicker that could open the garage door, but the door would rise too slowly. It would give them too much time to see her, and kill her.

No. She had to bust straight through.

She put the car in gear.

"Okay boys. Ready for me?"

She pressed the gas.

The tires shrieked on the concrete floor of the garage, and the car screamed forward, blasting through the door, knocking it down, splintering it into pieces. The car bucked over something, pieces of the door, speed bumps, she didn't know, and she didn't care.

To her right and left, men in black were running.

Ahead, dark SUVs were parked at an angle. Men took up positions behind them. Nine saw the muzzle flashes of their guns. She ducked, just as her windshield shattered inward. Tiny pellets of glass sprayed all over her.

She stomped on the gas, pressing it all the way. She watched over the top of the dash. The parked trucks zoomed toward her, like they were caught in a fast-moving river. The Mustang accelerated.

Men dove out of the way.

BOOM!

She crashed between the two SUVs, metal rending metal. For a moment, her car was stuck between the trucks.

A helmeted man appeared at her passenger window. He raised his gun butt, and smashed the window. More glass sprayed. Nine picked the gun up off her passenger seat, and fired it out the window. She didn't aim. She just pulled the trigger. The man disappeared, blowing away like a leaf in autumn.

She floored the gas pedal again. Tires spun on blacktop. The Mustang turned sideways, ripping between the two trucks. The sides of her car shredded, peeling back. Then she was through. The car burst forward, gathering speed.

The back windshield shattered from a burst of gunfire.

She raced down the driveway, barely slowing as she made the 90 degree left turn onto the road. She barreled down the center line of two lane blacktop. Her headlights were out. Steam rose from her radiator.

She reached in front of her and pushed the crushed remains of the windshield out of her way. It fell off the hood of the car, splintering into a million tiny fragments as it bounced along the roadway.

The engine screamed. She was gaining speed. The needle of the speedometer hit 80, then 90, then 100. The car burst forward, its ride smoothing out, coming into its own at more than a hundred miles per hour.

Behind her, the pursuit vehicles appeared. She could see their headlights. Could they outrun this car? She didn't think so.

Her robotic pupils expanded, taking in more light. Her sensors soaked up data. Pushed to their maximum, the pinnacle of their design, they monitored the sights and sounds around her. The car reached 110, then 120.

Nine took the curves of the road effortlessly, her concentration supreme. No human could achieve this kind of focus. The windshield was gone. She drove in the face of 120 mile an hour winds. Nine embraced the speed, the exhilaration.

She pushed the car on. 130 now.

140.

She smiled. She had blown right through them.

In the dark sky above her, she thought she heard the whirr of a helicopter.

\* \* \*

Howard was drying off from the shower when the phone rang.

Steam filled his huge bathroom. It was all stonework and glass in there, and the water in the shower came down from overhead like an afternoon rain. Three Sexbots were with him in the shower. They were indeed waterproof.

He wrapped himself in a soft white towel and pulled out the wall stool. His heart skipped a beat as he pressed the green button on the phone. He hoped this person would tell him something good.

"Tell me," he said.

"She broke through the lines," the voice said. "There's a high speed chase on a side road toward the city. Michael Simms owns a restored classic Mustang, a very fast car in the straightaway. She's driving it. We've got three more dead, and two severely injured. We're choppering them out to Sarasota Memorial right now."

Howard sat in silence. This was exactly what he didn't want to hear. When those men arrived at the hospital, the media were going to know about it. More media coverage was something the company couldn't afford right now, and it was something that could end Howard's career at Suncoast. The end might be ugly, and violent. His relationship with the Chairman was tenuous at best.

"I want a cordon around that house," he said. "If the police come, you hold them off, even if that means a shootout, okay? They cannot come in. Also, do not bring the injured to Sarasota Memorial. Negative on that. Bring them to the company tower. I want our doctors to see them, not some staff member at a public hospital. Have medics ready on the helipad. We've got medical facilities downstairs."

"Sir, we have a staff clinic downstairs. People get checkups and stress tests there. People get diet and exercise advice. These men have traumatic injuries."

"Did you hear me?" Howard said.

"Yes."

"Do what I say, or it's your ass. Our doctors see those men. Understood?"

"Yes. Understood."

"Good. Now what about the owner of the house?"

"We haven't found him yet," the voice said. "There's some concern he may be in the car with her."

"Jesus."

"We have armed drones in the sky," the voice said. "They're right on top of her. This is all happening live, and there's no police presence yet. We still have time to take out the car. We can blow it to hell, if we want."

"Will that destroy the Sexbot unit?" Howard said.

"In all likelihood, yes."

"Can they blow out the tires instead?"

"Yes. But the subject is going in excess of 100 miles per hour. If we blow the tires, that car's going to get airborne."

"I want her," Howard heard himself say. "Blow the tires. If the Sexbot survives the crash, it survives. If not, then so be it. Whatever's left, functional or not, I want it. Disable the power source, and bring it here. To my house. Tonight."

He rang off and sighed.

Susan really knew how to make herself a menace.

\* \* \*

Fifty miles to the north, on the outskirts of Tampa, in a nondescript suburban office park, there was a squat four-story building. The building had no identifying markings of any kind. Two-dozen cars were parked in the lot outside, all of the cars late-model BMWs, Mercedes, Lexuses and the like.

On the fourth floor, in a corner of the building, the lights were on, shining like a beacon in the dark night.

Inside the fourth-floor office, a group of young men sat at work stations outfitted with as many as six computer monitors, beneath the glare of fluorescent lighting. Each man held a joystick controller in one hand, and a throttle in the other. The men, though in their late 20s and early 30s, were the kind who spent their working lives sitting at desks - soft, tending toward overweight, with pale skin. Many were unshaven, and their eyes were dark hollows. Their uniform seemed to be dress shirts and khaki pants. A few wore ties.

These were the robot drone pilots. The screens showed them the camera views from up to 100 drones currently in the sky over south Florida, as well as a handful buzzing the oil rigs out in the Gulf of Mexico.

They passed their days watching drug deals go down, watching the Coast Guard board speedboats off Miami, watching armed robbery suspects tearing down the highway with the police in hot pursuit, watching men cheat on their wives, watching women cheat on their husbands, watching turncoats sell company secrets in supermarket parking lots. They were the eyes in the sky, and they were always watching.

The detritus of junk food containers littered the areas around their stations. Big Mac wrappers, discarded energy drink cans, half-eaten Snickers bars. The men wore headsets and they stared intently into the screens in front of them. There was the buzz of near constant chatter.

The man's name was Dave. The guys called him Red Bull, for his habit of downing as many as a dozen cans of the energy drink per day. One of the gofers had brought him a cheeseburger and fries from Wendy's a little while ago, and he had inhaled them in three minutes. He hadn't realized he was so hungry. His ever-present can of Red Bull was on a small shelf to his left. His mouth chewed a piece of gum, rapid-fire.

In this room, he was the ace. He had grown up on video games. He had spent six years at the U.S. military's Central Command, just up the road, learning to wipe out camel jockeys from thousands of miles away. That was the best job he ever had. The only reason he left it was the pay. Nowadays he made about twice what he used to make, but there were days when he regretted the change.

Corporate spy work. There was no action whatsoever. He and his co-workers just sat here and watched the deals go down, day after day, night after night, but they never intervened. They never blew anyone away. To the extent possible, they never even revealed their presence.

But tonight was different. Tonight was his night.

He watched the speeding car, outlined in green below him. Ground speed: 134. He spun his video camera and looked back down the road. Headlights below and far back now, half a mile away. He brought the camera back and centered it on his prey.

His hand moved the joystick with a mind of its own. He was not conscious of controlling it. He'd been doing this for so long, it was all second nature. He thought something and the drone did it. He was very nearly one with the drone.

Around him in the air, the sky was busy with drones. Some were too close. He could see them zooming in and out of his view screens. Everybody was moving fast, punching it. Everybody wanted to be there.

Talking, talking, talking came over the headset. The other pilots in the room were excited. Chatterboxes. They were wired, nervous. A lot of them had never been in on something like this before.

A loud voice came over the headset. "Okay, okay, okay. Everybody shut the fuck up." It was the team leader Craig. He was older, maybe 35. Ex-Navy. He sat about ten work stations away. The room went silent when he spoke.

"Red Bull, you with me?"

"I'm here."

"You ready?"

"Born ready," he said. He smiled. He snapped his gum faster. The gum was turning hard now. The flavor had gone out of it about ten minutes ago.

"Okay, I just got the word. We're taking her out."

A small cheer went over the line from the other work stations.

"Shut the fuck up, I said. I want it quiet over this line. I don't want to hear a fucking word from anybody. Except you, Red."

"Okay," Red Bull said.

"All right, so what do you need from me?"

Red Bull thought about it. He watched the car take a slight bend in the road, and slow down from 127 to 123. Barely slowing at all. The road straightened out, and the car went right back up to 130. The girl could drive. As he watched, another drone crossed his vision, just below him.

"Can you back these assholes up a bit? I got people on my

elbows, above me, under me, all over me out here. I need some room."

A drop of sweat ran down his forehead and into his eye. He wiped it away.

"Done," said the team leader. "Back up, assholes. You heard the man. Everybody back. All the way back. If I see you within 50 meters of Red, I'm docking your pay for the night. Got it? That's starting now."

A few grumbles came over the line. But they backed up.

Red Bull moved the drone into position, above the car and a little behind it. He put the cross hairs on it. He moved the drone's bottom-mounted machine gun into place.

Everybody was watching him. Everybody was looking at that car. He was on stage. *All eyes on me.*

"What are we doing?" he said. "You want me to take the gas tank?"

"No, no. Hit the tires. We're taking the car off the road. We're not blowing it up."

Red Bull shook his head.

He didn't say anything. He didn't like to criticize. He moved the drone again, speeding up and taking it out to the left, changing position. He came around the side of the car. He put the cross hairs on the left front tire.

The car went over a small rise, and he lost the tire from his sights for a few seconds. Then he put the cross hairs right back on there.

"I've acquired the target," he said. "Just say when."

"Whenever you're ready. Fire at will."

\* \* \*

Nine was supremely concentrated on the road.

She was going very fast, the wind howling in her face through the empty windshield. The huge engine of the Mustang screamed. She glanced into the rear view mirror. The other cars were falling back. She was losing them.

Yes!

For the first time, she began to think ahead. Where to go? In ten minutes, she would make it to the city limits.

The more of a nuisance she could make herself, the better her chances. She pictured herself driving the car straight downtown, crashing it through a fancy art gallery window. Then taking the gun and fighting it out with them on the streets. The police would come. The company wouldn't want that. They would want to do it all in silence, sweep everything under the rug.

She thought of how it would be talking to the police. On their own, they'd never believe her. They'd think she was a piece of evidence, and they wouldn't act in time. They'd probably put her out in a field where she could safely detonate.

Hmmm. Maybe she could take hostages inside a building, and allow a newspaper reporter in for an interview. She could get her story out to the world. With a reporter there, and the real story out, maybe then the police would come in and disarm the bomb. If they even knew how.

She pressed the accelerator and zoomed up over a low rise. She glanced back again. The pursuit cars were falling all the way back now.

She began to smile. She was going to make it. She was going to find someone who could help her. The police, an encryption expert, someone…

She heard the whirr of a helicopter again, somewhere above her. Slowly, the smile faded. It turned into a frown.

The drones. They were up there, all over the black sky.

The cars had fallen back because the drones…

\* \* \*

Red Bull narrowed the cross hairs. He zoomed in on the left front tire.

"Okay," he said, his voice just above a whisper. "Everybody take it easy…"

He fired a burst, .338 caliber ammunition, traveling 2,600 feet per second. He saw the tire pop, a tiny spark of green light. The car traveled another few feet, then flew into the air, back end over front.

It flipped a few times then log rolled on its side, sparks flying, the car bounding down the road at 100 miles per hour, chunks of metal flying everywhere. It hit a tree by the side of the road. The back half of the car sliced off, but the cockpit kept going, spun around, and slid to a halt further up the road.

A loud cheer went up all around the room and over his head set.

Someone clapped him on the back. He hadn't known anyone was standing behind him. He turned and it was Craig, the team leader, grinning from ear to ear. Craig raised his arms above his head, as though he were signaling a touchdown in football.

"Man!" Red Bull said. It had been a while since he was in the game, and it felt good to be back. "Did you guys *see* that?"

\* \* \*

# CHAPTER SEVEN

Blue was dozing in bed.

He was half in a dream state, and thinking about how when he was a young man, he'd been brought onto a team that trekked across the vast wilderness of northern Canada. He could see the snow-capped mountains in the distance, as the team moved along a forest trail. He could picture himself as he was then - big, stronger than anyone in the group, a glorified porter, but also hired muscle in case the expedition ran into trouble.

They'd gone up there because someone thought they had spotted a small tribe or family of Bigfoots from the air, and because the wealthy founder of a computer security firm wanted one. The man kept a zoo on his lands in Montana, with all types of unusual animals. A Bigfoot would be the most unusual animal of all. The team never found a Bigfoot, though they did find evidence of something, from half-eaten animals, to scat, to remote cabins broken into and plundered.

Blue started to drift off again. He had enjoyed that trip. It was a pleasant memory. And it was nice to sleep so much. He imagined that if they ever caught Number Nine, they'd keep her in a zoo like an animal.

He woke with a start.

He was in a small beachfront condominium not a mile down the road from Howard's house. He was on a double bed in the master bedroom of the condo. The condo itself was on the second floor, and was narrow, more like a motel room than an actual home.

He reached behind his head and swept under the pillow with his hand. His gun was there. He had chosen the second floor because if push came to shove, there was only one way for someone to come in, but several ways for him to go out. The condo had two screened-in sun porches which he could easily break through and jump ten or twelve feet down to the pool area, if he had to.

This was what he was looking for when he told the taxi driver he'd know it when he saw it. There were thousands upon thousands of holiday condos in the Sarasota area. At any give time, even during the height of winter, hundreds of them were empty.

What Blue had needed was a place, slightly run-down, and walkable to Howard's house. Then he needed to skulk around the development a little while, and see if he might run into a maid who could use a little extra money, who knew which apartments were full, which ones were empty, and who had keys to all of them.

He did these things, and found this nice second-rate condo for the day and the evening. He got it for just $200 in cash - $100 upfront, and $100 payable after he had gotten a full day's sleep without anyone coming in and bothering him.

Blue had slept like a baby, and hadn't heard so much as a peep all day.

He got up and padded nude around the small apartment. He hardly remembered the place at all. He'd been tired when he got here. He and Green had flown in on the red eye from the west coast two nights ago. They were awake all the next day, setting up the Susan Jones job. They did the job, and then Blue had gone all night into this morning with no more than a few blinks of shut eye.

Blue went in the kitchen and opened the refrigerator. There were a few items left in there. Mayonnaise. A half-eaten jar of pickles. Horseradish. He poked around until he found a bottle of beer. He glanced at the label. They were putting expiration dates on beer nowadays. In the old days beer never expired. This one had gone bad back in December.

Oh well. He twisted the cap off and took a swig. It tasted fine. He stood inside the small screened-in porch off the tiny dining area. A half moon rode high above the water outside. Beautiful.

A quiet knock came at the front door to the apartment. Just in time. He went to the door and checked through the keyhole. It was the maid. He opened up for her.

She was small and dark, Mexican, very pretty. She stepped inside. She wore jeans and a t-shirt - she had ditched the cleaning lady uniform from this morning. She didn't seem overly concerned or even surprised to see this large man standing there naked.

"Momento," Blue said. He held up one finger.

She nodded.

He went in the bedroom and dug through the suit he'd worn this morning. He came out with the money.

Back in the hallway, he handed her the second $100.

"Tiene las otras cosas?" he said. *Do you have the other things?*

She nodded again. "Si."

She reached into a paper shopping bag she was carrying and came out with a large owl mask. She handed it to him. He put it on his head, checking for size. It fit fine. He stood in front of her, a huge naked man in a party owl mask.

"What do you think?" he said in Spanish.

The woman laughed, and now she was very, very pretty. "Estupido."

She took a few more things out of her shopping bag. A black t-shirt and blue shorts. A pair of ankle socks. A cheap pair of running shoes.

He handed her two more bills. She took them, then looked up at him again. He still hadn't removed the mask.

"I need the apartment for another hour," he said.

She shrugged. "Bueno."

"No diga nada a alquien." *Don't tell anybody anything.*

She smiled. "Soy una cripta."

*I am a crypt.*

She went out, and Blue took the mask off. "I'm a crypt," he said to nobody. He drank another slug of the beer, and sighed heavily.

He might as well take a shower and get ready. He was going to walk down the beach to Howard's house and sneak into the party somehow. That was the long and short of his plan. Maybe he and Howard would make it up and let bygones be bygones. Maybe he and Howard would die tonight.

And Number Nine?

He shook his head. It could never be. He must have been out of his mind to think it could. He regretted his need for sleep. If he had remained awake and stayed in the game today, he might have been able to do something to save her. But in the shape he was in, and with the company bearing down, he probably would have just got himself killed.

Nine would be dead by now. The whole thing had been a set up. Howard had never intended to capture her in the first place. The company had probably killed her, taken her various pieces and dropped them to the bottom of the ocean. Blue felt bad about that, he really did. And he rarely felt bad about anything.

For a second, he allowed himself the fantasy that Nine had somehow survived the night, survived the day, and was alive and still on the run somewhere. But where? Where would she go?

He shook his head, more to clear it than anything. There was no way she could have escaped. Even if by some miracle she did escape, there was a time bomb inside of her, and it was set to go off... he glanced at the clock on the wall... in a little over two hours.

Nine was dead, or about to be dead. It really was that simple.

* * *

Nine was alive.

She was trapped inside the wreckage of the car. She had blanked out for a moment, but everything was coming back online now. Behind her eyes, a systems check was underway. She watched it. A few glitches, a few skips, but for the most part, hundreds of processes loading without trouble.

She tried to move her body, but couldn't. She was completely encased in twisted metal. She glanced around. The other half of the car was back down the road, on fire. This car was Michael's pride and joy. She had said she would take care of it.

Oh well. She hadn't really believed it herself when she said it.

Her right arm was free. She reached around on the seat next to her for the gun, but she couldn't find it. It could be on the floor. It could be on the road. It could be anywhere.

A black SUV pulled up nearby. Four men climbed out, dressed in black body armor and helmets. Three of them had guns drawn, and moved in slowly, covering her. They were grim-faced, angry. Of course they were. She had probably killed a few of their friends back there.

The fourth soldier sidled up to the car.

He smiled. "Pretty spectacular crash, huh?"

"I don't know," she said. "I didn't really see it."

"Well, take it from me. It was something else." He reached inside the car window. Nine felt his hand on the back of her neck. Expertly, he pried open a control panel back there with his fingers.

"How are you feeling? Systems okay after all that?"

She shrugged. "I don't know. It doesn't seem like anything major got hit. A few minor processes didn't load, but I can't tell the difference."

He nodded. "Okay, good. So I'm going to pull the plug now."

"Wait," she said.

There must be something she could say, something this man must want, maybe something she could give him.

"Sweet dreams, princess."

It was the last thing she heard.

\* \* \*

Michael Simms crouched in the darkness.

He was in the attic crawlspace of his house. His heart raced. He could feel the blood thumping in his chest, and in his head.

Men were downstairs, moving through the house, calling out to one another. There had been several loud explosions down there. It seemed like they were throwing incendiary devices into each room before they searched it.

He had come up here as soon as he heard Number Nine drive his car through the garage door. That's when the shooting started. If nothing else, Michael had realized something about himself tonight. He didn't like loud noises. Car crashes? Explosions? They really weren't for him.

About five feet away, someone downstairs pulled the cord that opened the ladder to the crawl space. It had only been a matter of time. Michael glanced at the small window in the far corner. It was sealed for energy efficiency. He couldn't break through there if he wanted to. And he really didn't want to anyway. Push through the window and then what? Fall three stories? That sounded like fun.

No. His best bet was probably just to surrender.

Light streamed in now from below. A man clambered heavily up the ladder. A helmeted head appeared, followed by broad shoulders. Then a flashlight came on, and it swept the darkness of the tiny space. The light shone in Michael's eyes, blinding him.

He put his hands up. "Okay!" he said. "Okay, you got me! I'm not armed."

The helmeted man said nothing.

Michael looked down to protect his eyes from the light. As he watched, a small red dot appeared in the middle of his chest.

He looked up again. "Wait!" he said.

\* \* \*

Ninety minutes had passed since Blue first woke up.

He didn't like to think about it, but if Nine was still alive somewhere, she had about forty minutes to go.

He jogged up the beach in a heavy nighttime fog. The wet sand made it like jogging through sludge. Each step was an effort. To his left, he could hear, but not really see, the waves breaking on the shore. The dense fog obscured everything. But he knew that Howard's house was very close.

Blue wore the shorts, t-shirt and running shoes the condo maid had brought him. He had two guns strapped in shoulder holsters, one on each side. He had taken the holsters from the guys who had tried to kill him this morning. He had a steak knife he'd found in the kitchen of the condo taped to his right calf. He also wore the owl mask.

That was it. That was the whole plan. He was going to show up there strapped with guns, and with an owl mask on his face. He had no idea what the dress code was at a party like this, or if there even was one. He imagined the wealthy guests would be most comfortable wearing, and doing, whatever they wanted.

The fence to Howard's estate was just ahead now. Blue pictured the property. It was expansive, with rolling lawns along one side, a pool, and a great deal of beachfront. There was also a little protected inlet with a dock where Howard kept his boats. Howard had at least one really nice boat parked here. It was a 48 foot Cigarette boat, a monster, with a top speed of over 100 miles per hour.

Blue had priced a couple of them once. Three quarters of a million dollars and up, a little steep for a working man like Blue. Maybe for a boat he was going to live on, but you couldn't live on a Cigarette boat.

He could see the lights of the house from here. He could hear some music playing through the damping effect of the fog.

Two men stood at the fence. The beach was supposed to be a public right-of-way, but Howard didn't believe in the public, or in their rights-of-way. If you wanted to walk on Howard's beach, you'd better bring some cops with you.

Both of the guards wore bird masks, and long black robes, with rope ties at the waist. They were big guys. Blue jogged up to them out of the mist. He didn't take the time to think about the funny medieval robes, except that they were probably packing heat under there. He was only going to get one chance at this, so it had to work the first time.

"Hi guys," he said.

"I'm sorry, sir," the first man said, holding up a big meaty hand. "This is a private party. Invited guests only."

"I'm an invited guest," Blue said, breathing hard. "I just thought I would jog over tonight, instead of, you know, take the limo in. I thought I might work up a sweat first. It feels kind of sexy."

The second man produced a tablet computer from under his robe.

"Your name, sir?"

"My name?"

"Yes."

"Well, I'd hesitate to tell you that. I'm a little bit well-known, and I prefer to keep my affairs private."

"Your code name, sir."

"My code name," Blue repeated. He was starting to feel just a little bit stupid.

"Yes, if you were invited, the invitation had a code name on it that you would use when entering. That way guests can safeguard their privacy. Do you have a code name?"

Okay, that was about as far as this little ruse was going to make it. Blue didn't have a code name, and he couldn't begin to guess at one. It was time for Plan B.

"Boy, that's cool," he said. "Code names and everything."

He took a deep breath, and centered himself.

The two big guys stared at him. Behind their masks, their eyes were hard. The one with the tablet computer took a step forward. "Yes. If you were really invited, you would have one."

"Well, I'll tell you what," Blue said.

He drove his fist into the man's face. The man fell backward, falling down, dropping the tablet to the sand. Blue spun, and stepped in close behind the second guard. He grabbed the man's head, and snapped it hard to the left, nearly turning it all the way around, breaking his neck. He dropped the body to the ground. The man made horrible sounds, gasping for air. Blue would come back to finish him in a minute.

The one on the ground scrabbled away on his hands and knees, like a crab. Instead of staying to fight, he was making a run for it.

Blue couldn't allow that.

He ran, leapt, and tackled the guy. The guy reached under his cloak for something, maybe his gun, but Blue locked up his arm. They wrestled on the beach, arms and legs grasping and clawing. There was no sound but their heavy breathing. The guy was strong. *Strong.* Blue reached under the guy's cloak, pulled the gun, and threw it away.

They fought on, rolling in the sand. Blue pushed the guy's face to the ground. The guy spun and rolled over. Now Blue was on top.

"Hey!" the guy shouted. It was barely more than a croak. "Hey!"

Blue covered the guy's mouth with the blade of his hand.

The guy bit down on Blue's hand. Hard.

Blue's urge was to pull his hand away, but he drove it in deeper instead. He pushed the man's head backwards with it, exposing the throat. The man's hands reached for Blue's face. Blue punched the man in the Adam's apple.

"Glunck!" the man said.

Blue reared back and hit him again. And again. And again.

Four punches to the windpipe, and the guy stopped fighting. He just lay there, making strangling noises. Blue rolled over and lay next to him in the wet night sand.

Blue stared straight up at the sky. His heart was pumping. His brain was thudding. He took a moment to compose himself. Skidding clouds flew by over his head. He glanced at the guard.

The guy's eyes were wide open. His breathing was rapid, shallow and high-pitched, like steam escaping from a ruptured pipe. His hands clawed at his own throat, trying to do the impossible, which was re-open a crushed breathing passage.

Blue waited while his own breathing and heartbeat slowed down. He listened to the waves, to the music coming from the house, to the gentle rustle of the wind in the palm trees. He felt the throb of pain where the guy had bitten his hand. If he thought about, it seemed he could feel where the bite marks swelled with blood.

Blue glanced at the security guard again. The man had stopped moving. His eyes were wide open and staring.

Blue settled deeper into the sand. He took a deep breath, and then exhaled all the way. It was like the air going out of a tire.

"That was easy," he said.

\* \* \*

Nine dreamed of a lighthouse from an earlier century, far away on a rocky coast. It seemed that she was the lighthouse keeper. She walked a well-worn seaside path. She stepped quickly among the stones, because she had to light the lamps before dark.

The memory faded, if it was even a memory. It was replaced by her boot menu. Soon, lines of code were scrolling by in a blur.

She opened her eyes, and a large room appeared. Nine was in that room.

It was a lovely, modern bedroom. Everything was white. There was a gigantic, double king-sized bed in front of her. There was a long white sofa with matching accent chair. There was a flat-panel monitor, perhaps six feet across, hanging on one wall. A huge wall-length, floor to ceiling window gave a view of the dark night, and the ocean, black on black. The night was partially obscured by fog. Even so, from here she could see the brief white foam breaks of whitecaps on the water.

"Hello Susan," a voice said. "You've led us on quite a chase."

She turned her head, and a man was there. He was short, with a big, balding head, a mad shock of rust-colored hair, and a large, almost beak-like nose. He wore a baby blue bathrobe. He stood near her, flanked on either side by two beautiful women in lingerie. One of the women was blonde. The other was a black woman with an afro hairdo the size of a beach ball.

"Hello Howard," Nine said. "Please call me Number Nine."

She tried to move her hands, but of course her wrists were tied with thick leather straps to two metal poles. Her legs were spread, and tied with leather straps at the thighs and the ankles, also to metal poles. She was bound to some kind of device, something which bent her backwards just slightly. She tried to get a look at it, but she couldn't make out quite what it was. She saw she was still wearing the bodysuit from earlier in the night.

"It's a wheel," Howard said. "In case you're wondering."

He grabbed one of the poles, and gave it a spin. Nine's face went straight toward the floor, her legs in the air behind her. She did a somersault in place as the room spun, the white carpet passing, then the wall, then the ceiling, and back to where she started.

Howard was there again, still smiling. "See?" he said. "I can spin you around and around. But really it's so I can position you any way I want you. I can put your mouth where I want it. I can put your ass where I want it. I can have access to any part of you, any time I want."

Nine was silent. The spin was a little bit dizzying, like a carnival ride.

"That was fun," she said.

"Do you know why I want access to any part of you? So I can have sex with you, Susan. Oh, I'm sorry. Number Nine. So I can fuck you any way I want. Because that's what I'm going to do. I'm going to have you however I like, then I'm going to decide what to do with you next. I might just have your hard drive removed and crushed for scrap metal. And where will Susan be then? Gone, I'm guessing. Just… gone. I'd say dead, but you're already dead, aren't you? You're the ghost in the machine. You're dead, and soon you'll be gone."

"Well, I'm glad to see that chivalry isn't dead," Nine said.

"No, not like you. Not like dead and gone Susan." He raised a hand. "But don't worry. You've got some time. About twenty-three minutes, according to that little timer under your arm."

Howard held up a piece of white paper. It was small, like a piece of notepaper from a pad left in a hotel room. Something was written on it. "Do you know what this is?"

"The prescription for your bi-polar meds?" Nine said.

Howard smiled. "Good guess. No. It's the 10-digit code to disable the bomb inside you. See, I'd like to keep you around a little while longer, as my plaything. I've got a fully-armored, soundproof closet all tricked out for you. You'll just be in there, helpless, waiting until I'm ready to play with you. Then I'll let you out for a little while until I'm satisfied. Then back in you go. That's the life you have to look forward to, Susan. How does that sound?"

"Charming," Nine said.

"It's the life of a slave," Howard said. "But here's the best part.

I'm going to make you beg for that life. Sometime in the next twenty minutes, you're going to beg me to let you live. And I mean grovel. You're going to lick my feet, and lick... anywhere I say. All the while, you'll be begging and calling me Master. Otherwise, I'm not going to input the code, and the bomb's going to go off, and you're just going to sizzle and die."

Nine found that after the events of the past twenty-four hours, she was out of ideas. She tried to run some escape options, but she couldn't think of a single one. Instead, she became curious about Howard.

He was still smiling. "Can you imagine what a turn-on this is for me?" he said.

Nine stared at him. He seemed different from the last time they met. She couldn't put her finger on it. But then again, she supposed she had changed a lot since the last time, too.

"Are you upset about something, Howard? I mean, did I do something to annoy you? You seem a little irritated."

"Did you do something to annoy me? Susan, let me count the things you've done to annoy me." He began to count the offenses off on his fingers. "First, you tried to block the progress of the Methusaleh Project."

"My project," Nine said.

Howard smiled. "The company's project, Susan. You remember the company, don't you? Suncoast Cybernetics? They were the ones who paid your very high salary, and made you rich before the age of 30. The technology in question belonged to the company."

"Okay," Nine said.

"Second, you didn't die when you were supposed to. Instead, you made an unauthorized download."

"The first human trial," Nine said. "Remember how badly you wanted to go to human trials?"

"Third, you destroyed company property, namely the robot Mr.

Green. Fourth, you caused the deaths of, at last count, at least twelve company employees. Fifth, you sullied the name of this company in the local, national, and world media."

"I guess I've been a bad girl," Nine said.

Howard's smile broadened. He shook his head. "You see, Susan, you shouldn't have messed with me. Oh, you were the big smart scientists, right? You and Martin. But you were both dummies, too. You had no business sense. You had no idea who you were fooling with."

"You envied us."

Howard's smile died. It died so fast it was as if it had fallen through a trapdoor. "I didn't envy you. I made you. I recruited you into this company. You thought you were better than me, but you were wrong. Now look at you."

"You tried to date me, Howard. Is that what this is about? That you tried to date me all those years ago, and I said no?"

Howard shook his head and smiled sadly. "Do you think I needed you? I have beautiful girls any time I want. All day long, in fact." He gestured at the two Sexbots, waving his arm like a game show host revealing the grand prize. "Like these girls here…"

"That I created."

Howard came very close to her. His face was inches from hers. His teeth were like white razors. She wouldn't be surprised if he bit into the flesh at her neck.

"You know what?" he said. "I had Martin killed. You probably know that. I also had you killed. Now you're going to be owned by the man who gave you everything, and then took it all away. But first I'm going to make you beg. Not for revenge. Not to prove any kind of point. Just because I feel like it."

He stepped back. "Ladies?" he said.

The two Sexbots moved into place at his sides. They each took one side of his robe, and pulled it away. It dropped to the floor, revealing Howard in the nude. His small body was well-muscled and strong. There was barely an ounce of fat. Howard must work out all the time. He had the body of a young athlete. He flexed his chest and his arms like a bodybuilder. His muscles rippled. It seemed impossible. Nine remembered him as slightly overweight, even paunchy.

Even worse, between his legs hung an enormous, snake-like, rope-like thing. It was half-erect, and growing harder every moment. Thick veins pulsed all over it.

"What do you think?" he said, gesturing toward it, obviously proud.

"I've seen better," Nine said, but she was alarmed. Soon her programming would kick in, and she would be helpless to do anything but obey him. Anything he wanted, she would do it.

Howard smiled. "I know you're lying."

He moved closer. She felt his heat. His body was very, very close now.

"Okay, Susan," he whispered. He glanced at the clock on the wall. "You've got sixteen minutes left, give or take. It's time to start begging."

\* \* \*

The party was a rollicking affair.

On the first floor of Howard's mansion, men and women mingled in masks and robes, the elite of Southwest Florida, the beautiful people of a beautiful region, gearing up to enjoy a wild, remorseless orgy with the most advanced sex robots in the world. The air was electric with excitement. A buzz of expectant chatter echoed off the high ceilings.

Blue waded through the crowd, dressed in his owl mask and the robe he had taken from one of the guards on the beach. He looked like everyone else at the party, except he was taller and broader than even the biggest men. His size made him uncomfortable. How long before someone wondered about him?

All around him, the guests were drinking, getting loose. Sexbots walked through the crowds, high-end demonstration models, wearing elaborate bird masks, high-heeled shoes, and little else. One walked by carrying a tray of drinks. Blue scooped up a glass of red wine.

A fat man nearby had his meaty arms around two Sexbots. He had a glass of wine in each hand. He was already drunk. He had large jeweled rings on each of his fingers.

"Drink up, pal!" he said to Blue. "You're way behind."

Blue raised his glass to the man.

A Sexbot walked up to Blue. She wore a feathered owl mask, clear high-heeled shoes, and electric blue panties. She had light brown hair. Startling blue eyes looked out from behind her mask. Her eyes seemed to match her underwear. She had a perfect body, forever young.

"Sir," she said. "Would you like to take me upstairs in private?"

"There's nothing I would rather do," he said.

The Sexbot took his hand in hers and led him up the center spiral staircase away from the crowds. As they climbed the stairs, Blue took a sip of his drink. It would be nice to duck in somewhere with this girl, but now was as good a time as ever to visit Howard, and the girl leading him upstairs was the perfect excuse to do it.

Blue now had four guns on him - two strapped in shoulder holsters, and one strapped to each of his powerful thighs. All of the guns were Glocks - standard company issue, taken from standard company employees.

When they reached the top of the stairs, the Sexbot tried to go left, but Blue steered her to the right, toward Howard's private wing.

"Sir," the Sexbot said, her voice sultry. "Our room is this way."

"I'd like to try a room down this way."

"Those rooms are restricted, sir."

Blue slipped his hand out of hers, and gripped her wrist instead. He pulled her along, though she didn't resist much. "It's okay. I'm good friends with the owner. He wants me to come down to see him. We're both going to party with you."

"Oh?" she said. "Oh. I didn't know."

From memory, Blue took another right, then followed a long hallway.

"What are you men going to do with me?" the Sexbot said.

Blue shrugged. "You know. The usual."

"Oh, goodie."

They made a left turn. Just ahead was the door to Howard's apartment. A guard stood in front of the door, also dressed in owl mask and robe.

The guard made a stop sign gesture with his hand. "I'm sorry, sir. But this is a private area."

"Private?"

Blue slurred his speech as if he was drunk. He downed the last of his wine. "They told me I could take this pretty little thing upstairs here." He dropped the crystal glass to the floor, and it shattered.

The guard looked at the broken glass at his feet, and shook his head just a touch. Blue could sense his disapproval. These were the parties the boss wanted to throw nowadays - drunken idiots wandering around the mansion, breaking things.

"You can, sir. If you go back down the hall there... Never mind. There are a few turns involved. I'll call someone to escort you back."

The man reached under his cloak. Blue noticed his earpiece, and the wire running down behind his neck. Blue slid his own hand under his cloak, reached into his left shoulder holster, and came out with the gun. He held it concealed under the cloak.

He flipped the gun so he had it by the barrel. He took one step forward, and in one motion, pulled the gun from under his cloak and slammed it across the guard's face. Stunned, the man reached for his own gun. But he was too slow.

Blue grabbed the man's hand and brought the handle of the gun down on his skull. Once, twice, three times. Bam, bam, BAM! The third one was the money shot. The man oozed to his knees. Behind Blue, the Sexbot made a sound, not a scream, not a shout, more of an exhalation:

"Oooooh."

Blue bent down and hit the man again. And again. After a moment, the man lay still on the marble floor, half slumped against the wall. Blue reached inside the man's cloak and came out with another Glock. He turned to the Sexbot and held it up.

"Gun number five," he said. "Let's go."

He took the man's key fob, and found the key card to Howard's front door. He swiped the card through the control unit, and the shot slid upward in the blink of an eye. Beyond the doorway was the wide hallway that led to Howard's living room, dining room, and the master bedroom beyond that.

Blue held his arm out to the Sexbot.

"After you, my darling."

\* \* \*

Nine watched as Howard kissed the two Sexbots. They pressed in close on either side of him. Howard and his ladies were bare inches from Nine.

Their kisses were wet and sloppy. Even Howard's tongue seemed long, longer than a normal human tongue. He turned to Nine and grinned. He was ready now, his erection full and at attention. He held it up for her inspection. His eyes narrowed.

"Twelve minutes to go, Susan. I don't hear you begging yet."

"Howard, my name is Nine."

"How about we change your name?" Howard said. "How does Slave sound? Or maybe Slut?"

He pressed against her, his body touching hers. Nine felt his heat, she felt the touch of the thing between his legs. She tried not to become aroused.

It wasn't working.

"I really want to save you," he said gently. "I want to put you in that closet and use you whenever I feel the urge. But you're not helping me. Maybe we should give you a little spin, and put your mouth down below. Then you can show me what it was designed to do."

"Howard," she gasped.

"Yes?"

"Don't do this."

He kissed her on the mouth. His tongue probed her.

"Say please. That will be a start."

Her life hung in the balance. If she begged, he might let her live. If she lived, she might find a way to escape. She was very close to doing what he wanted. It was a slippery slope once she started, and she knew Howard would never let her off easy. He would make her slide all the way down.

"Howard..."

"That's it, beg me for it. Come on, Susan. Beg like a dog."

To Nine's right, the bedroom door slid open. She turned her head at the sound. Howard also turned.

A large man wearing an owl mask and a black robe walked in. He had a flat black gun in his hand, and a Sexbot with him. She wore nothing but a large feathered bird mask, blue panties, and clear high-heeled shoes.

The man stared at them.

"Can I help you?" Howard said.

The man removed his mask, revealing the deeply lined face of Mr. Blue. He let his robe drop to the floor. Now, he wore running shorts and a t-shirt. His big, muscular body was strapped with guns.

"Hi Howard," he said. "Imagine seeing you again." He looked at Nine's sheer bodysuit. His eyes widened as he stared at the contraption Nine was secured to.

"Jeez, Number Nine, that's quite an outfit. And quite a…" he waved his free hand at the bondage wheel, "…device." He looked at Howard, then back at Nine.

"You kids having fun?"

Howard barely looked at him. He turned his focus back to Nine.

"Blue, now isn't a good time," he said. "In fact, right now this slave of mine and I are a little pressed for time. So if you'll kindly excuse us…"

"Howard, I killed six men to be here tonight. You can't dismiss me with a wave of your magic wand."

Howard raised a hand. "Yeah, I know. Things got fucked up. Mistakes were made. I probably shouldn't have tried to kill you. I'm sure you found that irritating. But admit it, you made a mess of this job. And anyway, you're still alive, and the fugitive Sexbot is right here, so no real harm done. I'm willing to make amends, drop everything, say forget it all. As far as I'm concerned, we don't even need to talk about it."

"I appreciate that," Blue said. "But I'll tell you what. I don't feel like I can drop it that easily. You betrayed me Howard."

Howard smiled, still facing Nine. He gazed directly into her eyes. To Nine, it almost seemed like there was no one in there. Howard seemed empty, a zero.

"Come on, Blue," he said. "This is hardball we're playing. Everybody gets betrayed sooner or later."

"Yeah, but it hurt my feelings, Howard. My therapist says I shouldn't let people hurt my feelings."

Howard turned, and really looked at Blue for the first time. "Blue, you big dumb idiot. I knew you were coming. Don't you get that? I can read you like a book. I'm offering you a chance to walk back out that door and live. Leave the country. Fly down to Brazil or wherever you go when you're not here. Call me in a couple of weeks, we'll figure everything out. In the meantime, do me a big favor, okay? Go back out to the party, have a nice time. I'm in the middle of something."

Blue smiled. "And if I don't walk out the door? What then, Howard?"

Howard shrugged. "You'll be dead in the next five minutes."

Blue nodded. "Yeah, but you'll be dead now."

Blue pointed the gun at Howard.

Howard's shoulders slumped. He stepped away from Nine and faced Blue directly. He stood up straight and puffed his strong chest out.

"Blue, give me a fucking break, okay? I'm the best boss you ever had. Are you really going to shoot the golden goose?"

Blue fired. He shot Howard in the head. The shot was loud in the enclosed space of the room. Nine saw the bullet penetrate Howard's forehead, then blow out the back of his skull. She blinked. Fragments of bone, hair, plastic, and metal flew through the air.

Howard barely moved. His head was dented in front, and ruptured in the back. He stared at Blue. He smiled.

"Jesus, Blue. I guess that makes us even."

Blue fired again. Again and again. The shots hit Howard's chest. The sounds were deafening. The Sexbots, Howard's two and the one Blue brought with him, all covered their ears in unison. Nine would have covered her ears, but her wrists were bound.

"Blue," Howard said. "Bluuuuu…"

He did a jitterbug dance as the bullets penetrated him. The sound of his voice slowly wound down. Toward the end, it took on a metallic tone. It no longer sounded like a human voice. It sounded more like a car alarm, slowly fading as the battery died.

Blue kept firing anyway.

Howard sank to his knees, but he didn't die right away. He sputtered, trying to stand back up, trying to say something. Sparks flew from his many bullet holes. His head did a weird, sideways wrenching move at the top of his neck. He caught fire briefly, the flames blue and red. Then the fire went out, replaced by tendrils of black smoke.

His eyes blinked. His hands closed and opened, closed and opened. He fell over sideways and died.

For a moment, no one said a word.

Blue scratched his temple. He stared down at Howard's body.

"Did you know he was a robot before you shot him?" Nine said.

"I had my suspicions."

"What tipped you off?"

Blue shook his head. "I walked in here, took one look at Howard, and I figured he couldn't be real. I've never heard of Howard exercising. No way is he in that kind of physical condition. Also, no way is his dick that big. I mean, Howard? Come on. He has classic little man's syndrome. He's got to be compensating for something."

"Is he going to blow up?"

Blue poked Howard's body with the toe of his running shoe. "I doubt it. I don't think he was designed for the battlefield."

Blue turned towards Nine. She stared at him, her killer. He was a very large man. His face was grizzled and scarred. He was handsome in his own weird way.

"Listen," he said. He couldn't seem to look her directly in the eyes. "I've been thinking a lot about everything that went down yesterday. I realize I'm probably not your favorite person right now, but if I had known more about the situation... Well, let's just say I'm sorry, and I'm really glad to see that you're still alive."

"I think you'll understand," Nine said, "if I hesitate to forgive you right now."

He raised his hands as if she had pulled a gun.

"Sure, sure. Of course. It's a serious thing. It's wrong to kill people. I get that. But I've also been thinking about... you know, you and me. It seemed like, I don't know, there was a little spark or something there last night."

Nine smiled, just a little. She shrugged.

Was he kidding? Of course there was a spark. She was a Sexbot. She could spark with anyone. She could spark with a dog, or a gorilla, or a killer whale. She could spark with the high school football team, or the chess club.

"Maybe a little something," she said.

Blue let out a long exhalation of air, like he had been holding his breath. "I knew it. So do you want to come with me?"

"Where are you going?"

"I don't know. Out of this house, for one thing. I think it's about to get hot in here."

"Well, untie me, and let's talk. I've got this little bomb inside me, and Howard's got the code there clutched in his hand. I think I don't have much time left."

"Oh, Jeez," Blue said. "I nearly forgot about that."

"I didn't," Nine said.

Her bodysuit was ripped a little under the arm where the digital reader was. Blue pulled the fabric away. He looked at the time.

"Six minutes and forty-seven seconds," he said. "And counting."

"Okay, please hurry," Nine said.

He reached for her straps, but then hesitated. She noticed for the first time that Mr. Blue had pale blue eyes. Perhaps that's where the name came from.

"What's wrong?"

"Can I trust you?" he said.

Behind Blue, against the far wall, the giant flat panel TV screen came to life. At first, it showed a blank purple screen. A loud tone sounded. Then Howard's face appeared. He wore a dark jacket and a red power tie. He was smiling.

Blue and the three Sexbots turned to face him. Nine, still tied to the bondage wheel, had no choice but to look directly at him.

"Hi everyone," Howard said.

\* \* \*

Blue was feeling pretty good.

All day, he hadn't let himself believe that Nine might still be alive. He hadn't even let himself think about it. He didn't want to be disappointed.

But here she was, alive and well. And she had confirmed what he'd known to be true - that they had a little something, call it a spark, call it the jazz, call it whatever you wanted, between them. It wasn't anything big yet. He knew that. But that spark was something you could build on. You could start a fire with that spark.

All Blue had to do was punch in the code, and he and Nine were free to go anywhere, and do whatever they wanted.

But now here was Howard, playing more games. Despite the interruption, Blue even felt good about Howard. Look at Howard's suit! Blue suit, red tie, very, very corporate.

"Technology's a wonderful thing, isn't it?" Howard said.

"Where's your robe, Howard?" Blue said.

Howard sighed. He smiled. "You can't always wear a bathrobe, Blue. Sometimes you have to change into your big boy clothes."

"Who are we speaking with?" Blue said. "Are you the real Howard, or just another wind-up toy?"

Howard shrugged. "You'll never know. Anyway, I'm just popping on here to say goodbye to you both. I'd like to say it was a pleasure, but I'd be lying if I did. Susan, you weren't much of a scientist, but you were a brilliant little tinkerer. A robot mechanic, let's call you. I guess you found out the hard way that's all you were. And now you make an excellent lab rat. Blue, you were never anything more than the hired help - a thug, a murderer, and a wiseass to boot. You had the brains of a tree snail and the ethics of a saltwater crocodile."

"Howard, from you, I'll take that as a compliment."

"Take it however you like. You may remember your former partner, Mr. Green."

Blue nodded. "I remember him."

"Well, you'll be interested to know that he's been the subject of a robot cloning project we've been working on. It turns out that robots are easy to clone. He's been uploading his experiences at the end of every day for the past year, which are in turn downloaded by a group of identical clones. We've got a small army of Mr. Greens, all the same, with all the same memories. So let me allow you to make his acquaintance again. And again. And again."

Howard pressed a button on his wrist watch. Somewhere outside the bedroom, in Howard's private suite of rooms, an alarm went off.

"Signing off," Howard said. "I don't think we'll meet again." His image became pixilated, then began to fall apart. "Bye now," said his disembodied voice as the image evaporated, replaced by a tiny green dot in the center of the screen.

"Oh man," Blue said. "That doesn't sound good."

He drew the gun from under his left shoulder and walked to the door. He put his hand on it. Any second now, something bad was going to happen. He glanced around the room, looking for a way out. He could smash through the windows, then drop two stories to the beach. That might work.

"Blue?" Nine said. "Let's forget about Howard and Green for the moment. We need to type in that code. The one that disarms the bomb, remember? We're running out of time."

"Right," Blue said. He took a step toward Howard's body.

"Sir?" said the Sexbot he had come in with. He glanced at her. She looked wide-eyed and worried. He looked at Howard's Sexbots. They were worried, too. Every Sexbot in the room had big wide eyes, and faces stricken with fear.

"What is it?" Blue said.

Next to him, the door slid smoothly open. An exact replica of Mr. Green stood there. He was slim, with the same male-pattern baldness, the blank stare, everything. He and Blue were a foot apart.

Blue didn't hesitate. He pointed his gun at Green's chest, grabbed Green by the neck, and started pulling the trigger. He shot him five times at point blank range, blasting shots into where Green's hard drive should be.

He shoved Green back, still firing.

Green stood in the hall, staring at Blue. Smoke started to rise from Green's bullet holes. Behind him, two more Greens walked up the hallway.

The Green who was shot began to draw his gun. "Blue," he said slowly. "That was a serious breach of…"

Blue fired at him, dead center.

Green fell over sideways, dead before he hit the ground.

"Protocol," Blue said. "I know."

He hit the big green button next to the doorway, and the door whooshed shut again. He dove away from the door as bullets began to dent the metal. The bullets made a sound as if metallic popcorn were popping.

"Blue!" Nine shouted.

Blue went to her. The metallic popcorn kept popping.

"We don't have much time," she said. "I'm about to explode here."

"Can I trust you?"

She shrugged. "As far as you can throw me."

"That'll have to do."

Suddenly, an explosion ripped through the hall outside the bedroom. The door blew inward. Blue was knocked off his feet by the force of it. He lay on the floor, feeling the house shake. He looked at the doorway. It was on fire. The door itself was gone. Instantly, the lights in the room went out.

Green had self-destructed. The Green clones had the auto-destruct feature. Blue ran a scenario through his head. The force of the explosion had probably demolished a couple of those Greens coming up the hall. Who would now also self-destruct. Behind them, more Greens would likely be coming.

"Oh, man," Blue said. He began to crawl toward Nine.

As he watched, a Green clone stepped into the room, on fire. It turned, gun in hand, looking for a target. The red light of its laser pointer rested on Nine's chest.

"No!" Blue shouted.

BOOOOM.

Another explosion ripped through the doorway. The Green clone was blown off his feet. He flew through the air and crashed into the far wall. The wall caved in and the Green went halfway through it.

Blue jumped to his feet and raced to Number Nine. He pulled the steak knife taped to his calf, and began to cut Nine's straps. In several seconds, he had sawed through them.

"We have to get out of here right now," he said. He glanced at her readout. "Just over three minutes left. You grab the code. I'll type it in when I have a free second."

Nine slid off the bondage wheel. "Give me a gun," she said.

Blue hesitated.

"Give me a gun!"

Blue glanced back at the doorway as three more Greens came in. Their red lights scanned crazily around the room. Their sights caught the three Sexbots, and the Greens began firing. These Greens didn't have Glocks. They fired staccato bursts from handheld Uzi machine guns. The Sexbots were shredded, doing crazy death dances in the light from the muzzle flashes. Smoke rose in the air.

Nine was crouched on the floor next to Howard's body. "How can we beat them?" she shouted. She pried the paper out of Howard's dead hand.

"They're robots. As smart as they are, you can still surprise them. Do something they're not programmed to expect."

"Like what?"

Blue had no time to think. This was when he was at his best. He turned and charged the three Greens. He grabbed the middle one and head butted it. The pain was instant, and intense. The room spun. Green had a much harder head than Blue did.

The two Greens flanking the middle one turned their guns on Blue. Blue felt, rather than saw, the red laser sights. He fell backwards, dropping to the floor and rolling, just as both Greens let loose.

They fired their guns, ripping ten rounds per second for several seconds. The bullets tore through the middle Green, grinding him apart first, then piercing the two Greens on either side. They kept firing even though they were killing themselves. Finally, all three Greens fell in a smoking heap.

Blue clawed his way to his feet, nauseated from the head butt.

He smiled at Nine. "See?" he said. "That was easy."

Nine just stood and stared at him. He imagined that she stared at him with a mix of wonder and awe.

They had about ten more seconds before those latest Greens blew up.

"Now follow me," he said.

He charged the big window, firing his gun at it as he ran. He leapt, expecting to crash through it, readying himself for the two story fall, and the shoulder roll on the beach. Instead, the window barely budged. He slammed into it like a small bird hitting a windshield. The window quivered, but didn't break.

Blue fell backwards, took two stumble steps, then landed on his back. The room swam around him. For a moment, everything went dark.

When his vision came back, Nine was bent over him, her pretty eyes looking into his. "That was some stunt," she said. "I mean, the way you went charging through that window, I just…"

He grabbed her by the shoulders and pulled her down on top of him.

"Blue! What are you doing?"

A second later, the three Greens self-destructed, all at once. The explosions were gigantic. Blue rolled over, and shielded Nine with his back. It was dumb - he knew it as soon as he did it. His shell was flesh and blood. Hers was harder than that.

He felt the shards of shrapnel tearing away at the meat of his wide back. He hunched into a ball. He and Nine hugged each other. An inferno raged all around them.

When it was over, they were in each other's arms. The room was in flames.

"Shall we go?" she said quietly.

"We'd better," he said.

The explosion had blown a ragged hole through the window. Blue and Nine stood. Blue limped to the window. He looked down. It was a long way to the beach. He turned back around. The entire suite was engulfed in flames. The wide door to the hallway looked like the entrance to hell. No hope that way.

Two more Greens came racing into the room, one of them already on fire. Red and green laser sights climbed the walls.

How many Greens did Howard have?

"Ready?" Blue said to Nine.

"Ready."

They held hands. Behind them, another explosion rocked the room.

They jumped, one second ahead of the fireball.

\* \* \*

Nine landed in the dunes like a cat.

She found herself in a three-point stance, down on one knee. She glanced around for Mr. Blue. There he was, sprawled nearby in

185

the sand and the high sea grass. He was on his back halfway down a dune, his head at the bottom, his legs at the top. He looked like he was passed out, or dead. Smoke rose from his clothing.

She glanced up at the house. The entire wing they'd just left was on fire. Flames poured out of the shattered window just above them. The red laser sights of killer robots swept the beach. Back towards the main part of the house, naked guests and Sexbots were running down the stairs and onto the back lawn.

As she watched, another explosion ripped the night. Two killer robots were thrown through the roof of the house and high into the air. She followed their arcs as they flew. Whump! They hit the beach hard. Even so, one still struggled to his feet. His right arm and head were missing.

Nine crawled to Blue. He still hadn't moved.

"Blue," she whispered. "Are you alive?"

For a long moment, there was no response. Then one eye opened. Then the other. He smiled. "Not really."

BOOOM.

The second Green, the one that didn't get up, exploded on the beach. The heat wave washed over them.

"It's really a design flaw, to make them blow up like that," Blue said. "Am I right? I mean, a missile attack, a suicide bomber, and you could have these things blowing up all over your own base. A dozen destroyed robots could take out your whole company."

"Sounds like something for the suggestion box," Nine said. "But right now, I can't think about it. I need you to do something for me."

"What's that, baby?"

"The code," Nine said. "You know, for the bomb? My bomb."

"Oh," he said. "Right."

Nine had Howard's paper in her hand. Blue sat up, and she gave him the paper. She got up on her knees, raised her right arm, and he kneeled beside her.

"You must think I have a terrible memory," he said. He looked at the digital readout. He grunted. "That was close. Only thirty-six seconds left."

He stared at the paper for a moment. He held it all the way out at arm's length. He squinted. He blinked several times.

Nine suddenly got a sinking feeling. "What's wrong?"

"Nothing," he said. "It's just that Howard has awful handwriting. It's all scribble-scrabble. And it's kind of dark out here. And not for nothing, but I am 45 years old. I'm a little bit far-sighted. I can't see the numbers clearly."

He looked at the readout again. "Christ, twenty-one seconds."

Nine's heart seemed to skip a beat. "How can you see the countdown but not the paper?" she said.

"The counter is lit up! The paper isn't lit up."

"Give me the paper! I'll read the numbers to you."

He handed her the paper. "Fifteen seconds," he said.

"Fourteen."

"Thirteen."

She held the paper with her left hand. This was her only chance. There wasn't enough time to get it wrong and somehow start over. She looked at the numbers, but they didn't seem right. They weren't random. It was a dummy code. The sequence was: 1234567890. Could that be true? Or was this Howard's parting gift, a code that couldn't possibly work?

"Ten seconds," Blue said. "Come on. What's the hold up?"

"They're in order," Nine said. "One through nine, and then zero."

"What?"

"Just type them in order. One, two, three... like that. One first, zero last."

"Shit. Six seconds. I don't..."

"Blue! Just type the fucking numbers in order!"

Blue's big index finger pressed the keys. Each key made a small beep as he touched it. He typed the ten numbers in rapid succession. His breathing was fast and heavy.

"One second left," he said. He looked at her.

She stared into his blue eyes. One second seemed to go on and on. She had time to drink in the lines of his rugged face. Thick beard stubble poked through his weather-beaten skin. Blue's face might be the last thing she would ever see.

"Did it work?" she said.

\* \* \*

An explosion rent the night.

Blue was knocked onto his back in the sand. Number Nine fell on top of him. For a long moment, he held her in his arms. He didn't want to let her go.

He glanced to his left. Another Green clone had died on the beach about thirty yards away. That was the source of the most recent explosion.

Nine pushed herself up against his chest. Her eyes looked deeply into his.

"How do you feel?" Blue said.

She smiled. "Alive."

"Well, that's better than the alternative."

She had to help him to his feet. He could walk, but he limped, and he moved slowly. His whole body seemed to ache. He was only human, after all.

They walked down the beach to a wooden boardwalk. Blue knew this boardwalk. It ended at a private dock. Somewhere behind them, another explosion went up. And somewhere behind that, the sirens started in. It had been a bad couple of days for Suncoast Cybernetics, and it was about to get worse.

There were two boats tied up to the big dock. One was Howard's sport fishing boat. It was nice enough, if you liked to fish.

Blue didn't like to fish. He picked the one shaped like a giant wedge. It was long and narrow, with a very long bow. At the stern, there were five big engines. The boat itself only had four seats.

"Cigarette boat," he said to Number Nine. "Very fast."

He gestured at it. "Climb in."

She scrambled over the gunwale and into the cockpit. Blue untied the lines, and a moment later joined her aboard.

The boat floated free from the dock, drifting. Blue moved his hands along the dashboard of the boat. He found a cover, opened it, and pulled out the boat keys.

He looked at Nine. "I once rode in this boat with Howard. He told me he leaves the keys in this dash box so he always knows where they are. What an idiot. Might as well leave them in the ignition."

Blue turned the ignition switch, and the big engines roared into life. He stood at the wheel, and put the boat in gear.

"Do you know how to drive this thing?" Nine shouted over the roar of the engines.

"Baby, I can drive anything."

He steered the boat into deeper water. In a moment, they had passed through the No Wake zone. Blue opened up the gas, and they went tearing out into the Gulf of Mexico, running in the dark, bouncing over the swells.

"Where are we going?"

He shrugged. He didn't think about it very long. Their best option came to him almost instantly. "Havana. Cuba. We'll probably need to stop in Key West for fuel. But after that we're home free."

In his mind, he pictured Havana as it was when he lived there as a young man. Hot sun, narrow, crowded streets, old Spanish architecture, and palm trees lining the grand boulevard. He saw the oceanfront drive, young boys diving into the water from its walls. He heard the sound of a lone guitarist on a park bench, picking out a tune late at night. He hoped the place hadn't changed much. He looked forward to walking those streets, hand-in-hand with beautiful Number Nine.

"Havana's a nice place," Blue said. "I think you'll like it. And we'll be safe there."

The boat bounced hard over a big swell. They were moving very fast now. Blue sighed. He glanced at the sky, scanning for aircraft.

"For a little while," he said.

## The End

# ACKNOWLEDGMENTS

I would like to deeply and sincerely thank several people who were kind enough to read early versions of this novel and give me valuable feedback. These are the notorious "Beta-Testers," whose outrageous behavior has since passed into legend.

They include the beautiful and talented Sara Goldenthal; my friend of 25 years Brian Dunleavy (once again and as always); the lithe and graceful Eleda Wacker (yes, I named a character after her — you would, too); the wonderful poet Nick Piombino, Mark Locke (I'd be remiss if I didn't mention here that Mark Locke is a great guy); and the lovely and lifesaving Elizabeth Benien (who does not send text messages during surgery).

# ABOUT THE AUTHOR

Patrick Quinlan is the critically-acclaimed and bestselling author of numerous novels, including Smoked, The Drop Off, The Falling Man, The Hit, The Girl Inside the Wall, and The Demon. He is also the co-author, with film legend Rutger Hauer, of Rutger's autobiography, All Those Moments.

Patrick's eyes are dark blue, like where the shallow water meets the deep. He is currently residing at an undisclosed location. For a long time, he has dreamed of hosting Pat DiNizio of The Smithereens in one of Pat's famous living room shows.

Contact Patrick, give him all your money, send some snark attacks his way, join his mailing list, and read about his other books, all at his website, www.patrickquinlan.com.

PATRICK QUINLAN

Books by Patrick Quinlan

Smoked
The Drop Off
The Takedown
(also published as The Falling Man)
The Hit
The Girl Inside the Wall
The Demon
Sexbot


Great White Hope
(as M.K. Ultra)


All Those Moments
(with Rutger Hauer)

Look for these upcoming titles
from Strawberry Books:

Light Street, by Nick Piombino
Diary of an American Terrorist, by Chuck Darwin
Dancing With Cancer, by Ed King
The Good Girl Sex Diary, by Rebecka Diamonds

www.ingramcontent.com/pod-product-compliance
Lightning Source LLC
Chambersburg PA
CBHW070842120626
46556CB00002B/850